A NOTE ON THE AUTHOR

Ratika Kapur's first novel, *Overwinter*, was longlisted for the Man Asian Literary Prize. *Elle* magazine's Indian edition included her in a *Granta*-inspired list of twenty writers under forty to look out for from South Asia. She lives in New Delhi with her husband and son.

The Private Life of
Mrs Sharma

RATIKA KAPUR

BLOOMSBURY

LONDON · OXFORD · NEW YORK · NEW DELHI · SYDNEY

Bloomsbury Paperbacks
An imprint of Bloomsbury Publishing Plc

50 Bedford Square
London
WC1B 3DP
UK

1385 Broadway
New York
NY 10018
USA

www.bloomsbury.com

BLOOMSBURY and the Diana logo are trademarks of Bloomsbury Publishing Plc

First published in Great Britain 2015
This paperback edition first published in 2016

British Library Cataloguing-in-Publication Data
A catalogue record for this book is available from the British Library.

ISBN: TPB: 978-1-4088-7364-9
        PB: 978-1-4088-7365-6
        ePub: 978-1-4088-7366-3

2 4 6 8 10 9 7 5 3 1

Typeset by Manmohan Kumar
Printed and bound in Great Britain by CPI Group (UK) Ltd, Croydon CR0 4YY

To find out more about our authors and books visit www.bloomsbury.com.
Here you will find extracts, author interviews, details of forthcoming events
and the option to sign up for our newsletters.

For my parents: Kuko and Vipen Kapur

1

I was walking up to the ticket counter to recharge my Metro card when some man stopped me.

Where are you going? he said.

Can't you see where I am going? I said.

There is a line here, he said.

I am in the ladies' line, I said.

I can't see any ladies' line here, he said.

I was just going to tell him to mind where he pokes his nose when another man, a younger man, who was wearing a tie with thin blue and grey stripes, interrupted us. Forgive me, bhaisahib, this younger man said in a very calm, cool voice, but let madam go in front.

This was how I first met Vineet. This was almost two months ago.

Three days after that both of us were standing on the platform at Hauz Khas waiting for the train to come. He did not see me, but I could see him just ten or twelve steps from where I was standing, and I knew that if I fixed my eyes on him he would, after some time, look back at me. And he did.

Thank you for that day, I said.

He walked up to me slowly, as if he was a little bit scared. I am sorry, I did not hear you, he said.

Thank you for that day in the line, I said.

Then the train came. He smiled at me, and turned and walked to the end of the train. I got into the ladies' compartment.

Seven or eight times after that I saw him at the station on my way to the clinic. It was not every day, but at least two or three mornings a week I would see him on the platform at the Hauz Khas Metro station, standing straight and steady and smart, jacket, shirt, pants, tie, waiting for the HUDA City Centre train to come. Other men played with their phones or looked down the train tunnel or walked up and down the platform or stared at women, but Vineet always stood calmly in one place, like a statue of some great man, waiting for the train. I liked that. I also liked the way he dressed, and from the types of clothes that he would wear I thought that he worked in an office, some fancy air-conditioned office with cubicles and carpets in one of those new steel and glass buildings in Gurgaon. His pants always had one very nice pressed line in the exact middle of each leg and his shirts never had even one line, and at that time, before I knew anything at all about him, I thought that his shirts must have been taken to a presswallah in the locality, and not only that, but also that the presswallah must have brought them back on hangers, not folded.

One morning I was standing behind him at the x-ray machine waiting for my purse when something happened to me and I tapped his shoulder with one finger and said, Are you going to work?

He turned around very suddenly and looked at me, first at my face and then at my feet, and then he nodded his head and smiled. He was wearing the same tie that he wore the first time I met him, the one with thin blue and grey stripes. He told me afterwards that the brand was Zodiac and he had bought it from Shoppers Stop. It cost him almost one thousand rupees.

But I should say here that I am not a cheap woman. I hail from a good family, a well-educated family, my father actually had a BSc in Botany, and I don't talk to men without reason. From time to time men come up to me. Some will offer me a smile, some will try their level best to talk to me and some, I have seen, will allow their eyes to roam all over my body. But I just walk away each and every time. I should also say that Vineet is also not that type of man, the type of man who makes passes at women. I am quite sure about this. Like me, he also hails from a good family, and I knew this from the first moment that I saw him, and that is why when we met each other again at the station four days after that and he asked me if I would like to meet him at Barista in SDA the next Sunday, I said yes. Obviously I waited for one or two seconds, but then I accepted his invitation.

We met each other at Barista at eleven o'clock in the morning, I remember, and there was a lot of noise all around. Still, it was a nice type of noise, it was happy noise. There were some girls playing a board game, there were three old women wearing blouses and pants who were drinking coffee and talking as loudly as the girls sitting next to them, and in one corner, all by himself, there was a boy playing a guitar. It was the first time I had been to Barista.

We did not ask each other many questions, we did not talk too much. We watched young people and old people sitting around us, we looked up at the TV, which, I remember, was on one English news channel, and one or two times we looked at each other. We talked a little bit about the weather and a little bit about the news, and that was all, and as it is supposed to be.

After that day, after that outing to Barista, we have met each other five or six times, and always for very short times, for samosas at Shefali Sweets, for example, or for momos outside the station. And then, obviously, we meet each other on the Metro when we go to work, which happens, without any type of planning, two or three times a week. We hardly talk on the train, but I like it like this. Actually, there is nothing that I want to tell him, nothing that I want to hear from him, and maybe this is odd, but the truth is that I am happy to just stand quietly next to him and look out of the window at the tops of the trees and buildings that pass by. When I am near him I feel calm. I feel like I feel when I see photos of snow.

And, as it is supposed to be, we have come to know each other slowly, we have come to know each other like friends come to know each other. Since our first meeting he has told me some small and big things about himself. He always has a cold bath, even in January, he likes to eat uncooked paneer from Quality Dairy in Aurobindo Place, and the smell of petrol makes him vomit. Apart from that, Vineet Sehgal is thirty years of age and he has lived in Delhi all his life. He has a BA in hotel management, he works as a manager in a hotel in Gurgaon and one day he is going to start his own business, his own catering business. His father, who used to work at State Bank of India, died six years ago, and he lives with his mother in Shivalik. His shirts are not sent to a presswallah, his mother presses them. I saw a photo of her on the wallpaper of his mobile, a chubby, fair lady in a baby pink chiffon sari posing in front of Akshardham Temple. And, like me, Vineet has no brothers or sisters.

Obviously there are many, many things that he has not told me. I don't know, for example, why at thirty years of age he is still not married. I don't know if he sleeps properly at night, or if his mother opens the door with a smile when he comes back home in the evening, or if he likes to walk around in the mall. And I don't know if he cries. Still, some things I have also come to know on my own. I know that he is an ambitious man. From time to time he has talked to me about saving up money to buy a flat in Ghaziabad or Greater Noida, a nice new flat that has twenty-four-hour power back-up and water supply, a lobby and a children's park with a jungle gym and swings and a slide, and he says that if he sells the flat that he lives in just now, he will have enough money for the down payment, and if he manages to get a second job at a call centre, the salary from that job, along with his mother's schoolteacher salary, would be enough to pay for the monthly instalments. I also know from the way that he carries himself, from how he is always so steady, so quiet and steady, whether he is standing in one place and waiting for the train to come or he is sitting peacefully in front of me in a restaurant, I know that he is a man with a lot of confidence, quiet confidence, the type of confidence that normally comes with grey hair, the type that I have only seen in my father or Doctor Sahib. Sometimes I think that maybe Vineet Sehgal has an old heart.

Then last evening came and we went to India Gate for ice cream. He had walked up to me at the station on Wednesday and asked me if I would like to go with him for a short outing on his motorbike, which had just come back from the workshop. See, I was not born yesterday. I know what it can mean, I know how it can feel, to ride behind a man on a two-wheeler. I know how the man could slowly lean back into the woman sitting behind him until his body is pressing against her chest, while the woman's hands could move from the handlebar behind her to the man's waist and then finally rest on his thighs as she leans forward against him. But I also know that this can only happen if a woman allows it to happen, which, obviously, I would never ever do. And I know that he is a good man who would never ever play such games with a woman. So that is why I agreed to go out with him. I agreed to go out with him and I don't think that it was wrong.

Actually, I thought that Vineet would ask me some questions. I know quite a lot about him, but he hardly knows anything about me. He knows my first name and he knows that I work at a doctor's clinic in Gurgaon, but that is all, and so I thought that maybe he would want to know some more things about me. But even yesterday he hardly asked me anything about my life, my home, my family. It is a little bit odd. But maybe he is too shy. Or maybe he does not like to interfere in other people's lives. Or maybe he is just scared to know too much.

So we reached India Gate at around seven o'clock. On both sides of Rajpath the lawns were filled with people. All around there were children, children with their families, and there were couples and hawkers and policemen. And above the lawns, on our left and right, balloons, toy helicopters, flashing lights and hundreds of happy voices filled the air. We parked near the middle of Rajpath, where the ice-cream carts were parked. I remained sitting on the bike and he got off. The left leg of his pants had got stuck in his sock. I looked up the road, at the dark shapes of the Rashtrapathi Bhavan buildings, then I looked down the road at India Gate. Both ends of Rajpath were so quiet, and without light. Underneath the evening sky, both ends looked like paintings, the type of paintings that I have seen in Doctor Sahib's house. It was quite beautiful.

After some time we walked down to India Gate, without words. When we reached the police barrier we stopped. As I looked up at the monument I tried to count how many times that I had come here. My rough calculation was six hundred times, about forty times every year for fifteen years. I remembered how in the early days Bobby always had to be bought an orange bar or a balloon. At that time there were no police barriers. At that time you could park your scooter anywhere you wanted to. And then I remembered the last time I was there, standing just there in front of India Gate, one and a half years ago in November 2009. That was when the trip to the mountains, to Manali, was planned. It was planned for this summer, actually. We were supposed to be there just now.

What are you thinking? Vineet said to me.

Nothing, I said.

Please tell me, he said.

I want to touch snow, I said.

He looked down at his shoes for one second, then he looked up at me. I can't make you touch snow, he said, but I can buy you an ice cream.

I asked him for a Vadilal Chocobar, but he bought me a Feast from Kwality Walls, which not only had chocolate on the outer covering, but also one thick piece of chocolate inside, wrapped around the ice-cream stick. It cost twenty-five rupees.

Do you like it? he said.

Yes, I said.

As good as snow? he said.

I don't know, I said. I have not tasted snow.

I obviously did not want Vineet to know where I live so I told him that I needed to buy onions and that he should drop me at the vegetable seller in the market, which he did, and then I walked alone to my house. It was almost nine o'clock when I entered, and Papaji and Mummyji were lying on their cots in the hall watching some TV serial. I had told them that I was going to Sarojini Nagar with my friend Rosie, a very sweet nurse from the clinic, to help her buy some things for her daughter's wedding. They would not have understood if I had told them that I was going out with a man. So, I greeted them both, picked up the dry clothes from the veranda and went into the bedroom.

Bobby was lying down with his headphones stuck in his ears, listening to music on his mobile, his feet hanging off his folding cot and his eyes closed. All six feet of him were quiet and steady. Bobby is a big, strong boy. I only give him Mother

Dairy token milk because the cream in packet milk is not properly mixed in. I give him two glasses daily without fail and when he was younger I gave him three glasses. I poked him in the stomach. His eyes opened, he smiled for one second, then his eyes closed again. He behaves a little bit oddly these days. He says that he does not like school, but it seems that he has girl problems. So, I was folding the clothes and trying to talk to Bobby, trying to make him smile for me again, when suddenly my mobile beeped. I took it out of my purse. It was an sms from Meena, the name that I used to save Vineet's number. He wanted me to call him up. I deleted the sms then and there, and finished folding the clothes, and then I went into the bathroom and called him up.

Like me, Vineet was also whispering. Maybe his mother was nearby. He asked me if I had had a nice time, he was worried that maybe I had got bored. I told him that I had had a lot of fun, I told him that I had not had such a lot fun in a long time. And that was actually the truth.

And then suddenly he said, I like talking to you.

What did you say? I said, even though I had heard what he said.

I like talking to you, he said.

Thank you, I said. What else could I say?

It is the truth, he said.

Then I laughed.

It is cute how you laugh, he said. You laugh like a schoolgirl.

But I am not a schoolgirl, and he knows this. I am a wife and a mother of a fifteen-year-old boy. This he does not know. And he does not have to. Who is he to me? He is just some man who I saw on the Metro, and I don't know how but we started talking to each other, and I don't know how but we have become something that is a little bit like friends, and that is all. We go on short outings together. That is all. And he has not even bothered to ask me anything about myself. If he does ask me, which I don't think will happen because he seems to be the type of person who does not care about such things as your father's name, your husband's name, your address, your work and what not, but if suddenly for some reason he does ask me, I will tell him. I will tell him anything he wants to know. I will tell him everything. What do I have to hide from him?

Still, I know that I have to be careful not to take a wrong step. That is why I always say to Bobby, Watch your step. Watch each and every step you take. People will tell you to walk holding your head up high, but I think that you have to keep your eyes on the ground and watch where you put your foot. We hear it on the train daily, Mind the gap. When you get on to the train, Mind the gap. When you get off the train, Mind the gap.

My name is Mrs Renuka Sharma. I am thirty-seven years of age and a married lady. I am a respectable married lady who hails from a good family, and I have a child and a respectable job, and a mother-in-law and father-in-law. I am not a schoolgirl, and even when I was a schoolgirl, when I was Miss Renuka Mishra, even then I actually never did the types of things that other girls of my age did. There was no bunking school to meet a boy, or notes or love letters exchanged, or phone calls in the darkness when the grown ups were sleeping. And it was not that I could not catch the attention of the boys loitering around me. Actually, I was quite a pretty girl, quite a clever, pretty girl, and I don't like to boast, but the truth is that I did break some hearts in the boys' school on the opposite side of the road. Still, I think that I knew at that time, just like I know now, that such foolishness is timewaste.

2

I don't like Sundays. Actually, what I should say is that I don't like Sundays any more, not since my husband left and went to Dubai. I wake up each Sunday morning and there is no job to go to, there is nowhere to go to at all. When my husband was here we would go to meet his parents in Ghaziabad for tea. From time to time we would go to watch a film at Shakuntalam. And as long as it was not raining or too cold, we always went to India Gate in the evening. It is not actually meeting people or watching films that I miss, and there are hardly any benefits to such things anyway, but at least there was always some plan. There was always some reason to get out of the house, and I would wear a nice sari, and from the cupboard I would take out smart shirts and pants for my husband and son, which I would press again and lay out neatly on the bed, and they would wear these clothes and then we would go out. Now my husband works in a foreign country, so there are no outings, and my in-laws live with me, so there is nobody to go and meet, no reason to dress up, and on most Sundays we just sit in the house, Bobby, my in-laws and I. It is true that this is the day when I get some time to do a little bit of stitching or darning, when I can re-arrange the cupboards or clean the fridge. Still, how long do such things take? I try my level best to convince Bobby to come with me for a walk to IIT or the Rose Garden, or to go to India Gate for ice cream or to one of the malls in Saket. Sometimes he does agree to accompany me, but I know that he would prefer to sit in front of the computer or watch some stupid cooking show on TV or lie around with his headphones on. It also seems that he likes this girl with green eyes at the bus stop and he does not know what to do, because Bobby is actually just a good, simple boy, and so sometimes he just lies on the divan with a long face doing nothing at all. But children are like this these days. At least my Bobby tries to make his mother happy from time to time.

Still, I think that the main reason that I don't like Sundays is because I can't go to work. I enjoy work. I enjoy being busy, work-busy, which is totally different from being house-busy. When you are house-busy it is not only your body that gets tired, which is fine, but your mind also gets very tired. So, I work at a famous doctor's clinic in Gurgaon, and it is a good job. Dr Raghubir Singh is a world-famous gynaecologist and obstetrician. He sees patients at his clinic in the mornings, and in the afternoons and evenings he does surgeries and his rounds at a big private hospital, which is centrally air-conditioned and has all the latest machines. Doctor Sahib has medical degrees from grand, grand institutions like AIIMS and the Royal College of Obstetricians and Gynaecologists in England, degrees that are framed in fancy gold-painted wood and hung all over the walls of the clinic, and even though he is a male doctor, his waiting room looks like a bus station, filled with patients who have waited for weeks and weeks to get an appointment. And these patients are not the types of women you see on the Metro or in your local market. They, or their husbands, are all rich and have many contacts. They are ladies from big business families, or wives of politicians or Class One officers or multinational executives, or are themselves politicians or Class One officers or multinational executives. They are ladies who live in Gurgaon's poshest apartment complexes, which have twenty-four-hour power and water, and swimming pools and gyms, or ladies from localities like Vasant Vihar or Golf Links, or ladies who live in one of those white bungalows near Connaught Place. I know this because I meet them daily. I am the person who keeps all their personal information in files. But I should say here that Doctor Sahib also does quite a lot of charity work. Every Saturday afternoon without fail he goes to a village near Manesar, where he sees village women for free, and every Thursday morning without fail he gives free consultations at the clinic to poor people, poor people like ayahs and washerwomen, and wives and daughters of drivers and gardeners and watchmen.

I have been working at the clinic for nine years, since Bobby was six years of age. My in-laws and husband don't mind because the clinic is open from 8.30 am to 12.30 pm and so I am already at home when Bobby comes back from school. I also get free check-ups and treatment. It is a good job.

But the truth is that it is not my dream job. See, if my mother had not become sick and my father did not have to spend all of his income, almost all of it, on her medical bills, I would have been a schoolteacher, a respected schoolteacher in a big school here in Delhi. I had always dreamt of being a schoolteacher. My father also did. Obviously he believed that a girl has to perform all her domestic duties, but he also thought that a girl should work, and because of a schoolteacher's timings he believed that she could do both. My dream was to do a BEd degree, and my father, who was a very broadminded man, was even ready to send me to Delhi for my studies. But by the time I passed out from school we had no money, and my father actually suffered two heart attacks because of this, so I had to start earning a salary as soon as I could. I enrolled in a secretarial course, which I topped, and the truth is that even if I was studying for a BEd, I think that I could have been a topper. So, as I had planned, I got a job immediately after I completed the secretarial course. I could have worked as a secretary for one of the big lawyers or property dealers of Meerut, but I don't actually like the types of girls who work as personal secretaries. They can be quite cheap sometimes, quite foolish, flirty and cheap. And what is a secretary actually? Isn't she just a substitute wife for the boss? Like his wife, she provides tea and snacks for the man and answers the phone for him. Like his wife, she is his protector, keeping him safe from unwanted elements of the world outside. At home his wife protects him from irritating children, interfering relatives, uninvited guests. At work his secretary protects him from unscheduled patients, annoying pharma sales reps, unhappy employees. And I don't think that I need to tell anybody what else some secretaries do that actually only wives are supposed to do. I think that everybody knows. Whatever it is, I did not want to do any of these things and that is why I decided to be a receptionist, and I think that it was the right decision.

So, I worked as a receptionist at a small private hospital for one year that time when I lived in Meerut, before I got married, and now, here in Delhi. But I won't work at Doctor Sahib's clinic forever and ever. The truth is that I am not like those other women who have no ambition, who think that work is just timepass that will give them a little bit of pocket money. No. One day, when my husband and I save enough money, I will start a training academy for Office Management, Computer Proficiency, Personality Development and Grooming, Business English, everything. My father used to say that a person's determination is his real power. I have still not told my husband, but I am determined to have my own business one day.

But just now I work at Dr Raghubir Singh's clinic and it is a good job. I have many duties. I type out all the letters, which Doctor Sahib dictates to me because I know shorthand, and I should say here that this is one of the reasons why he respects me, because how many people these days actually know shorthand? I answer calls, I sign for couriers, I do all the filing of patients' forms and cards, and I take all the payments. I have to make sure that the servants keep the whole clinic absolutely clean, that not one stain or one dot of dust should be seen, because Doctor Sahib is very, very particular about that, and that everything from the floor to the ceiling should shine. Every Thursday I even make one of the servants use sellotape to pull off any fallen hairs on the carpet in the waiting room. It is also my duty to make sure that the office boys and lab assistants are doing their jobs properly. So, even if my designation is receptionist and even if some of the work that I do could be called secretarial, I am actually more like the office manager.

I can talk in English quite nicely. I went to an English-medium school, my father was very particular that I attend an English-medium school, and for four years I even studied at a convent that was run by proper Irish nuns, not those Malayali sisters from Kerala. My husband taught me Word and Excel, and I learnt a little bit of PowerPoint on my own, so I am also quite proficient with computers, and I am excited because last month Doctor Sahib said that he is going to buy a computer that will only be for me to use.

⌒

Bobby and I Skyped with my husband this morning. We have a computer in the house, a Dell-brand computer that my husband's friend bought on our behalf from an auction at the American Embassy, because he has some contacts there, so it is an imported one and not one of those cheap assembled computers from Nehru Place. Bobby spends most of his time on it, but I also use it sometimes. It has a webcam, and we use it to Skype with my husband every Friday and Sunday. We talk every Friday because my husband works in Dubai and, being a very Muslim type of place, that is the off-day over there, and Sundays, obviously, because that is when Bobby and I are at home. And from time to time, my in-laws also use Skype to talk to their daughter and son-in-law in Canada.

So, we talked to my husband today. First Bobby gave him some long story about why his marks in the last unit tests were so-so, and then I took the headphones to talk. My husband looked tired and I told him this. He said that he had had a very busy day at the hospital yesterday. Still, he tried to look happy as he has always tried to do, and he asked me about Papaji and Mummyji, and why Bobby's studies were suffering. He told me that he had gone for a long walk on the beach on Friday evening and that he kept thinking about me. I forgot to ask him if it was Jumeirah Beach, which is where he sometimes goes on Friday evenings and where, he says, the world's most beautiful hotels have been built. We did not speak for too long because he had to go to the hospital. He was wearing a light blue shirt and red tie. Even though he was tired, he still looked handsome.

My husband's name is Dheeraj Sharma. He is a physiotherapist at a government hospital in Dubai. He has been there for one and a half years, and earns a good salary that is totally tax-free. He saves most of his money because he shares a small, little flat with four other men and lives like a sadhu, and every three months without fail he wire-transfers money to my bank account.

Except for Rosie from the clinic, whose husband also works in Dubai, people are always saying to me, Oh ho, you poor woman, your husband is so far away! Oh ho, you poor woman, you must be missing him such a lot! Oh ho, you poor woman! and what not. It is true that he is far away, even though from Delhi it is faster to reach Dubai by air than to reach Chennai. And it is true that I miss him. But what can I say? We have duties. As parents, as children, we have duties. I could keep my husband sitting in my lap all day, but when my in-laws grow older and get sick, who will pay for the hospital bills? The government? It took my father-in-law four years of begging and bribing the CGHS and maybe ten years of his life to get the reimbursement for his prostate operation.

And what about my son's education? Bobby is a good boy and most of the time he gets around ninety per cent in his final exams, but what is ninety per cent today? Ninety per cent does not guarantee anything today. What these people who keeping poking their noses in my life don't understand is that today the cut-offs at all the good colleges are ninety-five per cent or more, and so maybe we will be forced to put him in one of the new private universities, and these places have very high fees that we would never be able to afford if my husband remained in India, even if you include my salary and the little bit of extra money I make, which is only from small, little cuts from one or two of the suppliers that we use at the clinic, normally from the man who sells us ink cartridges and printer paper, and sometimes from the man who provides cleaning and sanitation supplies, and I only make this little extra money when the price of onions goes up and, I swear on God and I swear on my husband, never ever at any other time because then that would be greedy and wrong. So we need to save up money for Bobby's BCom, because BAs and BScs are actually timewaste, and then we also need money for Bobby's MBA. Bobby has to do his MBA because he is going to work in a multinational company or an international bank. But admissions for MBAs are so competitive that he will have to take costly coaching classes for the entrance test. How would we pay for all this? Sometimes I want to ask these people, these people who go on and on with their pity, who make me seem like I am some stone-hearted witch, sometimes I want to ask them one question, just one simple question. When my in-laws' medical bills grow into lakhs of rupees, when my son has to do his further studies, who will save us? Will love and romance save us?

3

I saw Vineet outside the station on Tuesday morning. He smiled and walked up to me, and then we walked down to the platform together. The train was late and so we started talking. He is an intelligent man. He reads the *Times of India* in English every morning. He says that he also always reads the Business section. I am always telling Bobby about how important it is to read the newspaper. It greatly improves one's general knowledge, which is important for MBA entrance exams, job interviews and everything else. Vineet told me that the real estate sector is going through some very serious problems and until it is granted industry status, builders, developers and consumers, basically everybody, will suffer. I like to talk about such topics. I know that one day I will talk to my son about them. And then the train came. Vineet and I got on and stood quietly side by side as we normally do.

Before we got off the train he asked me if I would agree to have lunch with him. For two or three seconds I did not say anything. I had been a little bit troubled that night after our outing to India Gate, a little bit troubled by his behaviour on the phone. But what had he actually done? I like talking to you, that was all he said, and that was all he meant. He did not tell me that he would bring me the stars from the sky. He is not that type of man, I know it. Romance is of no interest to him because that type of love always slows you down on the road to success, and he would allow nothing, he would allow nobody, to slow him down. That is surely why he is still not married. It is the man who walks alone who walks fastest, and Vineet, I am sure, likes to walk alone.

So, I did agree and we met each other for lunch yesterday, Wednesday, after I finished work at the clinic. It was his off-day. In the hotel industry, he told me, Sundays and even gazetted holidays are never guaranteed holidays for employees except if you are very senior or you work in a department like Finance. He works in Food & Beverage or F&B. The timings are very long and you even have to work on Diwali sometimes.

Vineet came all the way to Gurgaon on his motorbike to pick me up. I told him to meet me at the IFFCO Chowk station, and he was there at exactly 12.45 pm, as I had asked him to be. We decided to go to DLF Place in Saket, even though I would have been happy to go to any mall at all. Malls bring peace to me. It is true that it is always nice to see those salespersons in the showrooms dressed in smart clothes and those beautiful displays in the showroom windows, but what I like most is the cool and clean of the building, the cool air and the clean floors. I walk into a mall not to buy things, because everything is at least thirty per cent costlier than what is in the market, and then everything is also fixed price so you can't even bargain. I walk into a mall not to buy things, but to find peace.

We had a nice time together. We sat near the fountains outside, even though it was quite hot, and we talked about various topics. Vineet was in a talkative mood. I asked him to tell me more about his job and he told me that the hotel he works in is called a boutique hotel, which basically means that it is a small hotel, but even though it is small, it actually has only twenty-one rooms, even then it offers every type of fancy thing that big business executives want, including a chauffeur-driven Mercedes. It even has RO-filtered drinking water in the bathroom taps. He said that there are people who travel such a lot for work that they actually get bored of five-star hotels and prefer to stay in these small but very fancy hotels. His guests are basically foreigners.

Food is the most important thing for a hotel guest, he said, and I am the person who manages it all. The kitchen, the restaurant and room service, I manage it all. And as the F&B manager, the chefs, the restaurant manager, the waiters, all of them report to me.

But can you actually cook, Mr F&B? I said jokily.

I could be the next MasterChef India, he said, with a big smile on his face. If I wanted it, I could be sitting with Akshay Kumar in his car outside Chic Fish drinking beer and eating tandoori chicken.

I laughed. But do you drink beer? I said.

Obviously not, he said.

Actually, I knew that he did not. Not that it matters to me, but I know that Vineet is not that type of man. My husband also does not drink alcohol, and he does not even smoke. He eats meat from time to time but never ever in the house.

⌒

Bobby was a little bit agitated and angry that I came back home at five o'clock because I normally come back from the clinic before two o'clock to give him his lunch. Still, my in-laws greeted me with love, as they always do. Mummyji even offered to make me a cup of tea. That is how they are, my in-laws. They treat me as a daughter. They treat me with love, with love and respect. My father used to say, It is one thing to command respect, and it is another thing to give respect where it is due. Maybe I am a respectable woman from a respectable family, but my in-laws also have big enough hearts to give me the respect that I deserve. This is a rare quality. But then my in-laws are rare people. Money, for example, means nothing to them. These days, when everybody is looking for the most profitable marriage alliances for their children, my in-laws chose me for my family background, not my father's bank balance. My father was a simple shopkeeper, he had a small, little textbook and stationery shop in Meerut, and whatever little bit he earned he spent on his daughter's education and his wife's medical bills. That is why he had nothing in the bank. Still, my in-laws did not mind. They did not want anything from him, not a microwave, not a Maruti, and I will never ever forget how when my father sent them sweets at our engagement time, they kindly accepted the sweets, but then and there they gave back the silver tray on which the sweets were sent. I will never ever forget that. How can I?

And I think I can say that in all the years that I have been married, seventeen years actually, I have also not given them any reason to complain. Even if I think very hard, I can't actually remember one word that I have said or one action that I have committed in all these years that has given them any pain. Maybe there was one time just after my husband left, when my mother-in-law walked into the bedroom one Sunday afternoon and caught me sleeping in my husband's shirt. She was disturbed by that, which I think was fully understandable, and she said that it was a little bit indecent and childish, and obviously it was, and I was ashamed of my behaviour, and I promised to myself and to her that I would never ever behave like that again. But except for this one time, I don't think that I have given any problems at all to my in-laws, and so if from time to time I do something like come back home a little bit late, as I did yesterday, they are not troubled by it.

Still, Bobby was a little bit angry that I came back home at five o'clock, even though I had told him in the morning that Doctor Sahib had given me some extra filing work to do and that I would be late. When I entered the house he was lying on Papaji's cot in front of the TV and refused to look up at me. And obviously he had not eaten his lunch. That boy is almost sixteen years of age, but one thing he won't do is eat without me. Bobby won't even eat with his grandparents. He likes to loiter around in the kitchen while I prepare his food, and my mother-in-law does not allow him to do that, and then he wants me to sit by his side while he eats, as I do almost daily, at breakfast, at lunch, at dinner. And why not? A child has to have action and fun, but he also has to have some type of steadiness in his life. He gets a lot of peace from it. If he cannot expect this steadiness from his mother, then who can he expect it from? And it is a privilege for a mother, for somebody who has, by God's grace, been blessed with a boy, to fulfil those expectations.

These days my in-laws are worried that Bobby has become too quiet, that he spends too much time just lying around the house with a long face. I have heard them talk about this on the phone with their daughter when they think that I can't hear them, and from time to time they even tell me directly. They think that he has become this way since his father went to Dubai. A boy has to have his father there with him, they say, especially at this age. I just keep quiet. In many ways my husband is a good father. He is not like other men, and he always did a lot for his son. In the mornings, for example, when he was still here in Delhi, he gave Bobby his breakfast while I prepared our tiffins. He also helped him with his homework and took him on outings. Still, a father is a father. A father is a man. Can he well and truly know just by the way Bobby holds his spoon at lunchtime that the girl with the green eyes at the bus stop has ignored him? Can he know just from how Bobby's toes will sometimes twist and bend in a very odd way that the boy has had a difficult time at school? Can he know just by looking at Bobby's eyes that the boy is sick? Can a father know everything that there is to know about his son, even without the use of his sight?

I agree with my in-laws that something is a little bit wrong with Bobby, but the problem is actually not as serious as they think that it is. It is not these one and a half years without his father that troubles the boy. What troubles him, I am sure, apart from the bus-stop girl and some problems at school, is that the three of us, Bobby, my husband and I, were supposed to be on holiday just now. Before Bobby's father left for Dubai in November 2009, he promised to come back to India this summer and take Bobby for a holiday to Manali. We were supposed to be in the mountains just now, we were supposed to be rolling around in the snow. But see, my husband's boss is a difficult man, he is an Arab, who, like all Arabs, my husband says, hates Indians, and even though my husband is due his annual leave, actually, it is overdue by more than seven months, this Arab won't approve his leave just now. Even though my husband gave him six months' notice as per the rules, the Arab told my husband that if he wanted to go to India now, then he should just buy a one-way ticket to Delhi and forget about coming back. Obviously my husband was very angry about this, he even threatened to leave his job and come back to Delhi, but I told him to be calm and to not worry about it. I have also explained to Bobby that his father is having a difficult time just now, but that things will be fine soon. Bobby is a little bit sensitive, but he is a good boy and he will understand.

Still, the day ended very nicely. It was Doctor Sahib's sixtieth birthday party and apart from all his family and friends, he invited all the clinic staff to a huge lavish dinner at a banquet hall at the Taj Palace Hotel. I asked Bobby if he wanted to accompany me and he agreed. I had to tempt him to come by telling him that there would be a huge buffet. Food, eating food, talking about it, always makes my son happy. Sometimes he tries to tease me by telling me how he wants to be a chef, but I don't encourage this type of jokiness and I tell him in my strict voice that cooking is fine as timepass, that it would make his future wife a happy woman, but that it is still only timepass and nothing else.

I wore my mother's pink and gold chanderi sari, and Bobby said that I looked pretty. That is the type of sweet boy that he is. And just for me Bobby shaved, and he wet his hair and combed it with a neat side parting, and even though he refused to wear a suit, he agreed to wear a smart shirt and pants. He looked handsome, very handsome. The truth is, and I don't like to boast, but the truth is that he looked more handsome than Doctor Sahib's son.

I have lived in Delhi for a long time, I have lived in Delhi for seventeen years, actually, but I don't think that I have ever been to a party like this before. It is still a little difficult to believe, but there must have been fifty different dishes at least, from fifteen different countries. And there were these chefs actually cooking in front of guests, cooking prawns and pasta and dosas and what not. Rosie said that they are called live stations. She said that this type of banquet would have cost Doctor Sahib four thousand rupees per person at least because it was a five-star hotel and also because they were serving alcohol. There were about three hundred people there. We don't need a maths teacher to tell us how much money Doctor Sahib has to waste.

And it is not only plenty of money that he has to waste, as my own son said to me after I took him up to meet Doctor Sahib and his wife. We had been talking to them for some time. They asked me about my husband, they asked Bobby about his studies and his career plans and what not. They were being very kind to us, I thought. Then, as we walked away from them, Bobby turned to me and said, Ma, have you noticed how these types of people blabber on and on?

So? I said.

They don't just waste money, he said. They also waste words.

I was a little bit shocked, not by what he had said, and he did say such a lot in less than ten words, but I was shocked by the idea that a child who still has so many years of growing up in front of him would think and speak like such a grown up. How is it that my young son was thinking with the tired, angry mind of somebody old? How was he speaking in those particular sharp, serious tones that only grown ups speak in? But my Bobby spoke the truth. A young crow actually is wiser than its mother.

I could not think of the proper words to say back to Bobby so I said, Let them be. Now you don't waste your thoughts on them. Then I quickly took his hand and pulled him to the pastries. The day, I can say, ended sweetly.

4

I am alone in my house. My in-laws and Bobby are at Feroz Shah Kotla watching a cricket match. My husband had surprised us with four tickets for an IPL match, for my in-laws, Bobby and me, four tickets that cost six hundred rupees each. Without telling us he bought the tickets online from Dubai and had them delivered to our house here in Delhi. But I did not want to go, so I said that I was tired and had to take some rest at home. Bobby's friend Ankit went instead of me. We did not want to waste such a costly ticket.

Instead of going for the match I went to Vineet's hotel this evening. For some time now I have wanted to see this hotel that he works in, this fancy boutique hotel that he keeps talking about, so I called him up last night and asked him if we could go today. Since everybody was going for the match I thought that this would be a good chance. He agreed then and there. Sundays are best, he said, because business hotels have very low occupancy on holidays.

And the hotel is well and truly something to be seen. From the outside it looks like a big fancy house with a big fancy gate, like almost all the other houses on that road. You would never guess that it is a hotel, there are no signs anywhere, and Vineet told me that this was done on purpose because it is actually illegal to run a hotel in a residential area. But then you enter, and then and there you realise that this is no house. You walk in and you feel like you have walked into some foreign country. It is beautiful, and so quiet and clean. There is soft music playing, and in the middle of the lobby there is a waterfall and all these different varieties of plants around it. It looks just like one of those Japanese gardens that you see in a calendar. One foreigner was standing at the reception. He was wearing a beige-coloured suit and he looked very smart. It was difficult to believe that there were just four people, the foreigner, one woman at the reception desk, Vineet and I, in that huge, huge room. It was quiet and beautiful, and empty.

Vineet took me up in the lift to look at the guest rooms. I entered the first room and I think that my breath stopped for four or five seconds. I could not believe the beds, I could not believe how the beds were made. Not one wrinkle, the bedcover and sheets all tucked in so nicely, all stretched tightly over the mattress. It actually seemed that they were stitched on to the bed. And the pillows. I have never seen such white pillows, and so many of them on one bed. All the rooms, he told me, have Wi-Fi. And all around there was this sweet smell of jasmine. In the rooms, in the corridors, in the lobby, even in the bathrooms, all around there was this nice smell. Vineet said that they put perfumed oils in the AC ducts. And then there were the bathrooms. What can I say about those bathrooms? They were so beautiful, the taps shone like silver and there was granite and glass all around, and everything was so clean, so clean, that I could have just lay down then and there on the floor and gone to sleep.

Only three out of the twenty rooms were occupied because it was Sunday and business travellers want to be at home with their families on weekends. It is also low season in the summer, Vineet said. So, we went all around the hotel. He even took me into one of the occupied rooms to show me the thinnest laptop I have ever seen in my whole life. Obviously the guest was not there. The woman from the reception, who is a friend of Vineet's, had told him that the guest had gone out for dinner. But this laptop, it was as thin as a news magazine, and I am sure that when Bobby completes his MBA and gets a job, I am sure that this is the type of computer that he will carry to the office. I wish that I could have shown it to him. And the guest also had this shiny red leather case that was only for carrying ties. I wanted to pick it up for my husband but it was too big to slip into my purse.

Then Vineet took me to the kitchen, and again, it was something to be seen. How neat and clean it was, and it had a fridge that was bigger than my kitchen! And they only have RO-filtered water. Everywhere only RO-filtered water. You can even drink the water from the bathroom taps. Vineet said that they have to do this because most of their guests are foreigners and they have very delicate stomachs. I thought that this was quite funny. Who has a bath with his mouth open?

When we finished looking all around the hotel we went to the restaurant near the lobby and Vineet ordered tea and snacks for us. He said that he did not have to pay for it, he said that senior staff are allowed such things from time to time. The woman from the reception, what they call the front office, came and sat down with us. Her name is Neha. She was friendly, but there was something a little bit odd about her. I did not like how she wore her sari. It was draped too tightly around her hips and chest. And she went on and on about how there were all these guests making passes at her, which, I suspect, was all just for Vineet's ears. I wanted to tell her that it is all about the way that you carry yourself. Even if I am a little bit plump, I also have quite a nice body, but no man would dare put a hand on my shoulder because they can see from the way that I carry myself that I would never allow them to do that. I also think that she was being a little bit over-friendly, asking me too many questions, asking for my mobile number, and blabbering on and on like a schoolgirl, even though she looked like she was at least twenty-seven or twenty-eight years of age. Still, maybe I am wrong about her. And Vineet says that she is a good person.

After tea we went for a drive in the hotel's chauffeur–driven Mercedes. Vineet is obviously a popular man because the hotel's driver very happily agreed to take us. He took us on the Jaipur highway so that I could see how fast the car can go. Because it was Sunday, there was not a lot of traffic, and how fast the car went! But more than that, how smooth it was. It seemed that we were racing two or three feet above the road. Maybe that is how it feels to be in a plane. And apart from

TV screens on the headrests, which I have seen before, and automatic windows and automatic this and automatic that, apart from all that, the owner's initials were embroidered on the seats. On each seat, like a fancy company logo, the letters R and K were embroidered in gold! The owner had actually asked the car company to do that, Vineet told me, in gold silk thread. Even though it was machine embroidery, and I know if something is machine embroidery from ten feet away, even then it was very nice. But I should say that for the price of that car, I would have preferred to buy a flat in Faridabad.

When the driver took us back to the hotel he did not just leave us on the road. He drove the car into the driveway of the property, stopped at the main entrance, came out of the car and opened the doors for us, then he got back into the car and reversed on to the road, then turned the car around and then reversed it back into the driveway so that the car was parked properly, with its front facing out on to the road, ready for the next trip. It was just the way Doctor Sahib's driver drops him to the clinic every morning.

⌒

But now I am back at home. Now I am alone in my house. My in-laws and Bobby won't come back from the match until after eleven o'clock. Now I am alone and it is quiet all around. I never knew that these rooms could be so quiet.

First I thought that I would use this time to clean the prayer room properly, because we don't allow the cleaning woman to enter it, and that after that I would sit down and look at different models for desktop computers on the Internet. Doctor Sahib has promised to buy me a computer and he said that I could choose any one I want as long as it is not too costly. But then suddenly I felt like doing nothing. I just wanted to enjoy this quiet. I just wanted to look at the black screen of a TV that is not switched on, just stare at this quiet.

I like this flat. Actually, I like it very much. We shifted here one and a half years ago when my husband left for Dubai. The flat that we lived in before, which was just one floor above this one, had only one big room, a bathroom and a kitchen, which was suitable for my husband, Bobby and me, but would have been too small to share with my in-laws. So, when it was decided that my husband would take up the job in Dubai and that my in-laws would come to live with Bobby and me, we shifted into this flat, which has one bedroom, a hall where my in-laws sleep, because they insisted that Bobby and I should use the bedroom, a kitchen, one bathroom and a veranda that we partly enclosed to make the prayer room. My father-in-law helps us with the rent. This, also, he insisted on doing, but then he gets quite a good pension from the government, especially after the Sixth Pay Commission.

One day I hope that we can buy this flat. It is in a very good locality. From here it takes only seven minutes to walk to the Malviya Nagar market and less than twenty minutes to the Hauz Khas Metro station. Water supply is also not a big problem, normally. And the neighbours are decent people hailing from good families. I have decided that if the day comes when we own this place, which can only happen if my husband works in Dubai for at least seven years more, then I am going to buy proper curtains, just like the ones in Doctor Sahib's house. In his house, actually, not only do they have curtains all around, but they also have these transparent lacy curtains behind each set. It looks very nice. I think that I will buy curtains for the whole flat, with different prints and colours for each room. Maybe I will even put curtains in the kitchen.

⌒

I am alone at night for the first time in seventeen years, for the first time since I got married, maybe even for the first time in my life because I cannot remember my father or mother leaving me at home at night-time, and it feels nice. It feels very nice, actually. Everything is so peaceful that I prayed again, at ten o'clock at night. Everything is so peaceful and quiet that I think that I could actually feel God tonight.

Still, just because I am enjoying this, it does not mean that this is how I always want it to be. I like being married, I like having a full house and a family. People today complain that marriage means forgetting yourself and living for others, it means getting your husband's tiffin ready before the sun comes up and washing your child's school uniform and serving hot chapattis to your in-laws. Obviously marriage involves cooking and cleaning, looking after the house, looking after the family. That is how it is, that is a wife's duty, and maybe, sometimes, it can make you feel tired. But marriage is also about two people who like to hear each other talk, two people who enjoy going on outings together, who can joke together and cry together. Maybe this is not the case in every marriage, maybe not in the marriages that you read about in the newspaper or in those marriages that they show in TV serials, but you will see it in many marriages. You will see it in my marriage.

My husband is my friend. Maybe he is even my only friend. When I was young I never actually had friends. Maybe I was too busy with my studies and housework to find the time to meet other girls, but on my wedding night I know that I made a friend.

The first ten months that we were married, before I became pregnant with Bobby, were a lot of fun. My husband had already been working in Delhi for two years, so when I shifted here he spent a lot of time showing me this huge city. In the evenings and on weekends, he showed me all the grand monuments of Delhi, all the markets, east and west and north and south. He never ever allowed me to cook on Sundays, and we went to Bazaar Sitaram for chhole bhature, Ansari Road for kachoris, Gole Market for samosas and all types of other eating places. We roamed all around, we laughed, we blabbered on and on. You would have to put sellotape on our lips to make us stop talking. And even after Bobby was born we still went on our outings all around the city. We just took him wherever we wanted to go. Normally, for most couples, all the fun is gone, their whole life is gone, after they have had a baby. It is almost as if one small baby, one small, little baby, enters into the world, into his parents' world, and in one second swallows that whole world up, and the only things that his Mummy and Papa can now think about are baby's food and baby's shit and baby this and baby that. Now, I think I can say that my husband and I were good parents, I think I can say that we are still good parents. Still, nothing, not even the beautiful son that we were blessed with, could stop us from enjoying ourselves.

But he could also be serious, my husband, because my husband is a good man. Even Doctor Sahib thinks so. He performs all his duties. I don't have a brother, and when my father passed away in 1998, my husband performed the last rites as a loving son. And as a loving husband, a loving friend, he was always there with me. I remember how much he cried. When we had gone to the hospital to collect my father's body and the attendant pulled the sheet back from over my father's face, a face hard and grey and I don't know how but still full of pain, when I saw that face I just sat down there on the floor of the morgue and cried, and when my husband saw me, it was the first time that he was seeing me cry because I hardly ever cry, I never even cried on my wedding day, but when my husband saw me I remember that he sat down next to me and also cried. And not only that, my husband also took care of everything. Bobby was not even three years of age then, but my husband would give Bobby a bath and feed him. My husband even tried his level best to cook our meals and clean the house for those first one or two weeks. That is the type of person my husband is, that is the type of friend he is.

I am also his friend, I think. He tells me that from time to time, and it seems that he is telling the truth. In the evenings, for example, when my husband was still in Delhi, after he came back home from the hospital and had his bath, he would lie down on the divan with his cup of tea, and leaning against me he would tell me all about what had happened that day, about problems that he was having with some other physiotherapist, about delays in purchasing medical equipment, and what not, and I would listen, and many times I would give him advice. And even though I am a woman, I think that he always listened to my advice.

Actually, I have helped him through many difficult times. Some years ago, for example, when his younger sister refused to get married, but she, Neelam, is, by God's grace, happily married now and expecting a baby in July, but when some years ago she was totally against the idea of marriage because she wanted to do an MSc in Biotechnology, and my in-laws were putting pressure on my husband to talk to her, to make her change her mind, who helped him through all this? After months and months of fighting and tears in the family without any positive results, even my husband's older sister could not do anything, who was the one who made her sit down one day and finally put some sense into her head? I basically convinced her that her husband-to-be was a broadminded man and that if she performed all her duties as a wife he would surely allow her to pursue her higher studies. And Neelam listened to me and agreed to the marriage. But actually, this was not her fate. Her husband thought that an MSc, or any other type of further studies, was timewaste, and did not allow her to pursue it. But at that time how was I supposed to know what type of man her husband was going to be? How was I supposed to know that he would be just like most other men? But at least I helped my husband and her family get her married, and at least this man allowed her to work and Neelam got a well-paying job in a pharma company.

Yes, I am my husband's friend. Even today, when he is sitting far away in Dubai, he is always asking me for advice, always seeking my help. What am I supposed to say to the boss about my leave? he will ask me. How am I supposed to tell my roommate that it is his turn to pay the power bill? And what not. I think about his problem carefully, then I tell him what to do. Like a friend.

But we were also lovers, my husband and I. There was a lot of friendship, there was a lot of fun that we had and pain that we shared, but there were times, many, many times, when we put all that away on one side, along with our clothes, and quietly got into our bed, while Bobby was sleeping peacefully on the folding cot in the corner. I don't like to boast, but my husband could never keep his hands off me. He actually thinks that I have the most beautiful bones in the world, and he is a physiotherapist so he has seen many, many bones in his life. He would keep stroking my shoulders, nibbling them, and he would always tell me that no type of exercise, no type of physiotherapy, could create the type of perfect shoulder joints that I have, and that they could only be a gift from God, God, the engineer of all engineers. Obviously now I am a little bit plump, and I have become plumper since he left, and these bones that he loved now hide under a thin blanket of fat, but I think that he will still want me when he comes back. Yes, my husband could never keep his hands off me and the truth is that I also could hardly keep my hands off him. We would switch on the washing machine, Neelam and her husband gave it to us before they had left for Canada, and it is a very good LG-brand semi-automatic washing machine, we would switch it on so that the sounds that the machine made could hide the sounds that we made from Bobby, and then my husband and I would get into bed. I can't forget those days. Even now, when I switch on the washing machine, which is only on the second and fourth Saturdays of every month, I think of those days. And from time to time I touch myself. And there is nothing wrong with that. A long time ago I read in one of the magazines at the clinic that masturbation, even for women, is normal and healthy, and a doctor wrote that magazine article. You won't grow hair on the palms of your hands as the nuns used to tell us in school. And, actually, many women masturbate. They are just too ashamed to say that they do.

I know all about sex. I have been married a long time. I even know about porn. Bobby thinks that I am a fool, he thinks that I have no idea that he looks at porn on the Internet. But I know that he does, and I know a lot about those dirty photos and videos and stories that he looks at, the types of things that all boys, and all men, even my own husband, look at these days. Man on top, woman on top, this style, that style, doggy style. I was not born yesterday. And I know how men think, I know what they want. At the clinic, for example, day after day men come in with their wives and take small, little plastic cups into the toilet to collect their semen. I think that some of those men think about me when they are inside the toilet. I see how they look at me.

⌒

It is not even ten thirty now, but it seems as if it is two o'clock in the morning. Everything is quiet. The only sounds that I can hear are the sounds from Outer Ring Road, the sounds of trucks and fancy fast cars. Only truck drivers and rich young boys are not at home with their families on Sunday night, and also those men who are far, far away working in some foreign country. But my husband told us this morning that his boss has promised him that he can take his annual leave during the Eid holidays at the end of August. This would actually be very good for us because my in-laws will be leaving for Canada next month for my sister-in-law's delivery. Neelam has already sent the plane tickets, which I don't think is wrong even if she is the daughter, because in this case the daughter has more money than the son, and these are modern times and today we know that the daughter is no less than the son, you see it on all those girl-child advertisements, and I explained this to my husband who was not very happy when my in-laws first told him about it. So, yes, my in-laws are going to Canada and they won't be coming back until October. It will be just like the early days. In exactly one hundred and one days' time, it will be just my husband and Bobby and me.

5

Bobby was sick. Actually, Bobby was very sick. Stomach cramps, vomiting, diarrhoea, one full week in hospital. The boy suffered, and when this boy suffers he wants his father. This boy always wants his father. But then every son wants his father. And the truth is that my husband is a loving father, a patient and loving father. Bobby knows his father's love, he knew it even when he was two weeks old. When he was a baby troubled by colic, troubled by night-time, troubled by car alarms and fireworks, Bobby became calm as soon as his father lifted him to his chest. That small, little baby, that small, little baby heart, felt his father's love.

Still, how could I have told my husband to come back just now? How could I have just called him up and asked him to come back home? He would have lost his job, he would surely have lost his job, and along with that we would have lost everything that we had planned for. So, I told my husband, as I had told my in-laws, that there was nothing to worry about, that Bobby had only got a bad attack of food poisoning.

And, by God's grace, Bobby is well and truly fine now.

But even if I had asked my husband to come back, which obviously he would have, and he would have jumped on to the first plane to Delhi, but even if I had told him to come, what could he actually have done? Could he have actually slept on that dirty floor of the general ward for six nights? Could he have washed his son's vomit off his clothes, off the bed, off the floor? Could he have fought with the nurses to change the IV drip? Could he have lived on tea and bananas for seven days' time? Maybe he could have done all this, I don't know. Maybe he could have spent hours and hours standing in line at the chemist stalls outside, maybe he could have run to call the doctor on that second night when Bobby just fell down to the floor suddenly. Maybe he could have stayed with Bobby for one or two hours so that I could have gone back home at least one time in those seven days to have a bath. Rosie from the clinic kept telling me to call him up to come back. She said that it would help me, that it would help Bobby. But how could I have done that? How could I have risked my husband losing his job?

Rosie has to know all this. Rosie has to understand such problems. My husband got the job in Dubai through Jacob, her husband. Like many Malayalis, Jacob went to work in Dubai so that he could earn a better salary, so that he could give his family a better life. And when I told her about all our money problems, she was the one who told me to tell my husband to speak to Jacob, who then gave us the contact information for the placement agency that got my husband his job. I should say here that it took me almost one year just to make my husband call up the agency. I can't live without you! he kept saying. I can't live without my family! I won't be here to see my son grow up. My parents are growing old. And what not. And Bobby would also cry and cry when he heard us talking about Dubai. No! He would say. No! Papa will not go anywhere! No! No! No! I sometimes think that it is actually a miracle how countries and companies survive when men rule them. But in the end my husband came to his senses. By God's grace my husband came to his senses and he called up the agency, and eight months after that he was working in a huge, modern, fully air-conditioned hospital in Dubai and earning a suitable salary.

Poverty is a type of punishment. And like so many other families, the poverty that my family suffers from is punishment for a crime that we did not commit. It is a jail, a jail. Now when you are stuck in this jail, you have two choices. You can just keep sitting, quietly sitting and suffering inside the four walls of your cell, or you can stand up and try your best to break those walls down. Both choices bring their own difficulties, bring their own pain, and Rosie knows this. Rosie also knows that one of these choices will bring some freedom. The only thing that you have to do is to look at your life with the right zoom setting, like on a digital camera. When you use the right setting, when you zoom out, it is very easy to see which choice is right. The problem is that people are so stuck on what is in front of them, they are so stuck in the present trying their level best to make sure that the present time is easy to live through, that they make wrong choices that will only bring bigger difficulties in the future.

That is what happened with my mother, and sometimes it makes me very angry. Not even one month after her thirty-sixth birthday she was diagnosed with breast cancer. She had always been sickly, but this was cancer. This was horrible. And she was so young. And I was only thirteen years of age. My father brought her to AIIMS in Delhi so that the best doctors could give her the best treatment. The doctors there said that they would have to do an operation to remove the lump, but they also said that with the operation and some rounds of chemotherapy after that, she had very good chances of survival. But my mother said no. No. Give me as many pills as you want, she said, but no knives, no needles! My father then took her to many different private hospitals both in Delhi and in Meerut, but all the doctors in all the hospitals said one and the same thing. Operation or death. Still, my mother refused to agree. No, no, no! she said. I remember how my father begged her, day in and day out he begged her. I remember how he made me beg her. Still, she listened to nobody. Not her husband, not her only child. My father cried. I had never ever seen him cry before, but during that time he shed tears like a woman. But the only thing that my mother thought about was the pain of the present, the pain of those knives, those needles. She did not think about the suffering that would come in the future, first her own suffering, and then her husband and child's suffering after she was gone. Maybe she did not suffer the pain of an operation, the pain of needles, the side effects of the chemo medicines, but in less than one year the cancer ate her up like a mad and hungry animal. My mother died eleven months after she was first diagnosed with cancer. She was four months younger than I am today. And sometimes that makes me angry, and sometimes the anger seems a little bit like that cancer.

But what does this horrible story tell us? What is the lesson here? You don't have to read a Moral Science textbook to know. My mother was granted a choice, just like everybody is granted a choice, but, just like most other people, she was so stuck in the present that she made the wrong choice. She made a choice that killed her.

Whatever it is, many years after that my husband and I made a choice, but we made a choice with our eyes fixed on some point in front of us, on the future, on our child's future. It is difficult just now, I can't lie. I am alone, I am tired, and my husband is far away. But this is how it has to be.

See, we tried. My husband and I tried our level best to save money when he was here. We worked hard in our jobs and we worked hard at home. My husband took the bus to his hospital, not his scooter, to save petrol money. And at least three times a week he stayed in the hospital until late at night to earn overtime. From my side, I ignored one empty womb hungry for more. I don't like to boast, but my husband and I could have produced a cricket team. But we decided to have only one child. And I know that people think it is because we could not have any more. Yes, that is how hard we tried. I rinsed out milk packets with water to make sure that not one drop was wasted, I cooked masoor dal day after day because moong dal was too costly, I put potatoes in every dish to fill up my family's stomachs, I even made small, little deals with some of the suppliers at the clinic. Still, we could not save one paisa. And we were so happy together, the three of us. We were well and truly a model family, the type of family you see in car advertisements on TV, even if there were only three of us. But we were still prisoners of poverty. We were happy together, but together we were jailed. And so the choice was simple. My husband had to go to Dubai to earn a better salary. Still, the choice was also difficult. We knew that we would have to make some big sacrifices. But only a fool believes that there is such a thing as an easy choice. Only a fool thinks that he can escape sacrifice and still get what he wants. As my father used to say, Without death there can be no heaven.

6

That front-office woman from Vineet's hotel, Neha, called me up. I answered her call only because I did not recognise her number. She said that Vineet thought that something had happened to me because he had not seen me at the station for ten days and I had not answered his calls or replied to his smses. He was very, very worried about me, she said, and that is why she called me up. I knew that I should never have given her my number. Even the first time that I met her I thought that there was something odd about her. What does she think? Why is she interfering like this? And what does Vineet think? So what if he has not seen me? Who is he to me that I have to call him up every time I see a missed call from him or reply to every sms he sends? The man does not even know that I am a married woman with a fifteen-year-old son, and Neha tells me that he is worried about me? It is such a joke. Worried about me? Do any of them actually know the meaning of worry? These people are like children, they behave just like children.

But then without a husband or wife, without children and in-laws, you are always a child, no matter how old you are.

I am tired. I am tired in my heart, I am tired in my mind. The truth is that worrying about people makes me tired. I can feed a person and I can give him a bath, and I can do it day after day. I can go all the way to Shahdara to buy the purest herbal medicines and run off to the Jhandewalan temple every evening to seek Mother's blessings. I have done these things. I have done these things for my husband, my son and my father-in-law. But these things only make my body tired, and my body can recover quickly. What is actually difficult is trying to understand what a person needs day in and day out. What is difficult is the worrying day in and day out. Is he fine? Why is he sleeping such a lot? Why are his eyes looking like that? And it never stops. It never ever stops. Like his father, and even his father's father for that matter, that boy Bobby will never ask for anything, never say anything at all. He will lie around the house with a long face, he will lie around with his headphones stuffed in his ears, but he will not speak one word. And so you spend every second of every day and every second of every sleepless night trying your level best to understand what he needs, what he wants, what he is feeling, trying your level best to find some signs in his voice, in his breathing, in his eyes. This makes me very tired. Sometimes I want to shout at him. Bobby! I want to shout. Give me peace for just one day so that maybe I could sleep in peace for just one night! But who am I trying to fool? I think that it will only be the sleep of death that will grant me that peace.

It is a little bit odd, but when I think about my mother's illness I can't actually remember feeling this tired. I went to school in the mornings, because my father never ever let me miss one day except when we brought her to Delhi, and then I came back home and cooked and looked after my mother while my father was at the shop, and even then I don't think that I ever felt this tired. For almost one year I fed my mother, sponged her, gave her medicines, and I was only thirteen years of age, but I never ever felt like this, and it seems that it was because of the type of person that my mother was. She was a simple person, and her demands were always simple and direct. Get me a cup of tea, Renu, she used to say. Press my legs, Renu. Help me sit up, Renu. The demands were only made on my body. The demands on my head and heart did come afterwards, obviously, but that was after she was gone.

Then there was my father, my father and his lifelong heart problem, his four heart attacks. I did not actually have to look after him. He would have a heart attack, admit himself into the hospital for three or four days' time, come back home, rest for some time and go back to the shop. He never ever let me go to the hospital to meet him, he never ever let me fuss over him at home. The only thing that mattered to him was that I went to school daily and did my homework daily. Still, I always felt tired with worry. I never had to attend to him, but I always felt tired. Why? Because this sick and quiet man never directly told me what he was feeling, he never directly told me what he needed, and so I tired myself thinking day in and day out about what he could be feeling, what he could need, what I could do. Even when I got married and shifted to Delhi I was still always worried. He did not allow me to come to Meerut to take care of him, and, obviously, he would never come and stay in his daughter's house, my father would not even agree to one sip of water in his daughter's house, so from far away in Delhi I just kept worrying about him. Day in and day out I used to think, Is his chest hurting? Is he breathless? Does he need better medicines? Is he dying? For years and years I remained tired, tired from thinking that any minute my father could die. And the truth is that it was only the night after my father died that I actually got my first full night of sleep.

But for how long could that peace last? For how long could my head and heart remain light enough that I could float through my days and sleep peacefully at night? After my father was gone, it was my father-in-law next. And in this case it was diabetes. Even now my father-in-law takes two insulin injections daily, and if he does not eat immediately after his injection, his blood sugar falls, and then he falls down to the floor, thud, just like that. He will not warn you of that sinking feeling, he won't tell you that he is feeling uncomfortable and needs to eat. No. And so, like with all these men, you have to be alert, you always have to be alert. You have to watch out carefully for signs, signs that don't come out from the mouth in the form of words, but in the small, little movements of the body, signs that demand your attention day in and day out. And now that he and my mother-in-law live in my house, in my care, it is my duty to understand his needs before he or anybody else does. It is my duty to make sure that he eats his meals on time, that there are always at least four doses of insulin in the fridge, and to keep all sweets and fried foods hidden from him as if he was a child.

And then, obviously, there is my real child, Bobby. But Bobby is fine now. By God's grace, Bobby is well and truly fine now.

But who will need me next? Who will I have to worry about next? Who else is standing in line waiting for my attention? I sometimes think that the head and heart that God gave me don't actually belong to me, that even though they live inside me, I don't actually own them. Sometimes I just want to shout. Give me back my head! I want to say. Give me back my heart! When I talk to my husband about this, he tells me that I have to learn to take a little holiday from all the demands in my life. He says that I worry about everything too much, he says that I worry without reason, and that the sky won't fall down if I sit down and relax for some time. And then he tells me that stupid story about the house lizards, about how two lizard-friends on the ceiling of a room were talking one day and one of them suggested that they go on a little outing. Absolutely not! the other friend said. Who will hold up the ceiling?

Maybe it is a funny story, maybe it is also a lesson for some people, but it does not apply to my life. Maybe the sky or the ceiling won't come crashing down, but if I took a little holiday, if I took two or three days off as my husband tells me to, my house would become a garbage dump, and in this dump my son would be starving to death, my father-in-law would be lying on the floor in a diabetic coma and my poor mother-in-law would just be sitting in one corner watching everything around her break down, until, obviously, she called up her son, who would jump on to the first plane back to Delhi, come back home and look at the mess helplessly, and then, when

I would come back from my little holiday, he would gently put his hands on my shoulders, and look at me and say, Renu, what have you done?

Still, my husband is probably right. From time to time everybody has to take a little holiday from his life, from all the big and small everyday things. Maybe that is why I enjoyed that evening alone at home when everybody went for the cricket match. Maybe that is why I enjoy meeting Vineet. During those times, all the small, little difficulties of everyday seem far away. When I am with Vineet it seems that I can just forget everything, everybody, just like that.

But how can I meet Vineet again? What would I tell him? Will I tell him that my son, Mrs Renuka Sharma's son, got drunk on some cheap country liquor with his friends and he became so sick that he was in hospital for one full week? Is this what I will tell him because this is what actually happened? It was not food poisoning. It was alcohol poisoning. Yes, alcohol. My sweet Bobby did not eat bad momos on the roadside. That boy drank alcohol. Alcohol. So, what will I say to Vineet? Will I say, Oh, did you know, Vineetji, that I have a son called Bobby? Oh, and let me tell you about something a little bit odd that happened ten days ago. Is that how I am supposed to start? See, Vineet, my son went out with some friends one Wednesday afternoon, then he came back home around seven o'clock in the evening and sat at the computer for some time, and then just like that he went to sleep quietly. And it was not even nine o'clock. He refused to have dinner, he did not even have a glass of milk. He just went to sleep. Then what would I say? Maybe I could tell Vineet how at ten thirty

Bobby suddenly woke up screaming in pain. He was suddenly screaming in pain, vomiting, running to the bathroom. First I thought that it was some type of food poisoning, something bad that he ate when he had gone out to the market with his friends. But when I saw blood in his vomit I became very scared. I quickly called up Rosie. She told me what medicines to give him so I ran to the chemist and bought all the tablets and gave them to Bobby, but then and there he vomited all of them out. He could not even keep one drop of water in him. Yes, I could tell Vineet about the buckets of vomit. And the pain. How my son kept screaming in pain, how he kept pulling my arm and screaming, Ma, do something! He was twisting around on the floor like somebody who is possessed, and screaming and crying, Ma, do something! I had never ever seen my Bobby like that. I did not know what to do. Then I finally called up Doctor Sahib. I told him what was happening and he told me to take Bobby to the emergency room at Safdarjang Hospital immediately.

My Bobby was in hospital for one week. One full week. One full week of stomach cramps, vomiting, diarrhoea, blood. What can I say? It was horrible. All around there was blood. All around there was vomit. And for the first two or three days the pain was so bad, so bad, that my Bobby could not lie down quietly even for one minute. He would sit up for half a minute, then stand up, then he would crawl around the hospital bed like a mad dog, like a mad dog mad with pain. So, am I supposed to tell Vineet all of this? Am I supposed to tell Vineet how the other two boys that Bobby was drinking with almost died, and how the doctors said that it was only by God's grace that my son did not have to suffer as much as they did? Bobby was drinking alcohol. Is this what I will tell Vineet?

Nobody in our family, not even my uncle who gambled, nobody has ever, ever touched alcohol. Not one drop. Am I going to tell Vineet about how my fifteen-year-old son drank cheap liquor like some cheap labourer? I could not tell my own husband, and, obviously, I could not tell Papaji or Mummyji. So how can I tell some man that I met on the Metro just because his stupid friend told me that he is worried about me?

$\sim$

I beat Bobby. I waited until he was fine, and I waited until Papaji and Mummyji went out for their evening walk yesterday, and then I beat him. I beat him with a man's hands. I beat him with his father's hands and his grandfathers' hands. It seemed that my hands had received their strength from all these men, it seemed that I was beating him on behalf of these men who were not here themselves to do the beating. Bobby said nothing. As I beat him, as I beat my words into him, he sat on the bed with his head down, and not one sound came out of his mouth. Not one sound. But Bobby understood. That boy understood in his bones that what he had done was horrible, horrible and shameful, that nobody in the family, not from his mother's side or his father's side, has ever touched alcohol, and that even though he was saved this time, if he ever went anywhere near that poison again his mother would break his legs. He also understood, he understood once and for all, that he could never ever speak about this horrible and shameful act to anybody, especially not to his father or his grandparents. And when I finished, Bobby quietly got up and left the room.

❧

I wish that I were twelve years of age again, when worry was just a word that you heard around you, not something that you suffered like a sickness. It was such a nice time then. I was only a reason for worry, and even then not very much because I hardly gave my parents any trouble. But I never ever had to feel any worry. My mother was still quite healthy then, when I was twelve years of age. She was still strong enough to press my school uniform, oil my hair and make my plaits, and cook, and sing to me. She was still strong enough to be a mother. And in those days my father was also a happy man. He used to walk me to school each and every morning, giving me mental maths problems along the way, and in the evenings he switched on the radio and helped me with my studies. A lot of people grow up, but they still don't stop being children. I stopped being a child at thirteen years of age, when my mother fell sick. I stopped being a child when I was still a child. But until I was twelve years of age, I lived without worry. And at that time I had only ten toenails to cut.

7

Everybody at the clinic was kinder to me than normal when I went back to work this morning after eleven days' leave, and this was because I had lied to them, as I had lied to everybody else, as I had even tried to lie to myself. I gave them the same sad little story about how Bobby had got a very serious case of food poisoning. If I had told them the truth, nobody would have spoken to me. Maybe I would have even lost my job. Doctor Sahib was very, very kind to me and called me into his room. I sat down on one of the patient's chairs opposite him, because he asked me to, and he ordered tea for me, which came in a white and pink teacup with very pretty flowers on it. Doctor Sahib actually looked very worried. He asked me all types of questions about Bobby, his diet, his stools, the colour of his skin, and what not, and he said that he could get me an appointment with the top gastroenterologist in Delhi if I wanted a second opinion. He even told me that I could take more leave if I needed it. It was very, very kind of him. I felt very happy. But then suddenly, just like that, he asked me if I needed money. He got up from his chair, walked around the table, sat down on the chair next to me and actually asked me if I needed money. Financial help, those were the words he used. Financial help, as if they would sound less like charity, as if they would sound less like an insult.

But I did not give Doctor Sahib a tight slap across his face because I knew that he did not purposely want to insult me. I did not leave the room and my job because I have seen, I have seen for some time now, that there are many things that Doctor Sahib and his type of people just don't understand. And I did not spit on him. I just said, Forgive me, Doctor Sahib, but I don't need any financial help, and then I started talking about one of the lab assistant's leave applications.

⟶

I left the clinic half an hour early to meet Vineet for a cup of tea at his hotel. It must have been forty-five degrees outside, on TV yesterday they said that there would be a heat wave this week, and there was a burning wind that was blowing outside, a wind that was like fire, but behind the clean glass walls of the Amaryllis Hotel it was like a February morning. Actually, it was so cold inside Vineet's hotel that I had to wrap the pallu of my sari around my shoulders.

We sat in the restaurant, which, except for one bearer, was empty. I told Vineet that I was sorry for not calling him up. I told him that I had been sick, and that was hardly a lie. A child's illness is also his mother's. As I talked about strong medicines, hospitals and doctors, Vineet listened to me quietly, his eyes small and serious and wet, as if I was speaking about death. As if I was speaking the truth. I felt bad, I felt very bad. In these three months that we have known each other, today was the first time that I actually lied to him. If he does not know that I am married, that I am thirty-seven years of age, that I have a child, it is only because he has never bothered to ask me. And I will never talk about things without reason, I will never talk about things without being asked about them. In all this time, he has never ever asked me about my family, and so I have not said anything. That is my only crime. Still, I felt bad. He is a good person, and as I talked I saw kindness in those small and serious eyes. So then I thought that I should tell him a little bit more about myself. What did I have to hide? But I had just started to talk, I was just going to say in a cool, calm way, with a bit of a laugh, because a laugh normally makes these types of situations a little bit less difficult, so I had just started to say, Oh, but you know nothing about me, when he said, Stop. He fixed his eyes on my eyes and said, Stop, I don't need to know anything more about you than what you want to tell me.

I should have felt relieved. My body, which felt as if somebody was holding it from top and bottom, and twisting it into a tight coil like a dupatta, my body should have loosened, but as long as his eyes remained on my eyes, every muscle in me remained tense.

It is like this, he said, looking inside his teacup. A person should never demand more than he is given. Supposing somebody gives you an envelope with fifty-one rupees in it on your birthday. You don't say, Uncleji, can I have a little bit more, please? Do you?

I was quiet. The truth is that I liked what he said. But then it is so easy to say deep and pretty things. The question is whether he can actually live by all this poetry. I will wait and see. I will wait and see how long it takes for Vineet to finally break, to finally break and hit his fist down on the table and demand from me all the facts of my life. But until that happens I will not allow myself to be carried away by his poetry.

So, I remained quiet and he also did, until Neha entered, floating into the restaurant like a heroine from a hit film. She came up to us, hugged me like I was her sister and sat down at our table.

A crow trying to walk like a swan, that is what I think when I see her. Everything about her is imitation. The way those lipsticky lips move, the way those hands move when she is saying something, when she is saying anything at all. And those imitation diamond studs in her ears. All of it is fake, and I suspect that all of it is for Vineet.

After she sat down, Neha looked at Vineet, then at me, then at Vineet again, and then she squeezed my hand and said, Thank God you have come. You don't know how worried this poor Vineet has been. Actually, she did not say this. Actually, she sang this. I have seen that Neha does not speak. She does not speak properly like you and I speak. Her words come out like songs, cheap love songs.

Vineet turned his face to the window.

I am telling you, Neha said, I have known this boy for almost two years but I have never seen him behave like this before. He was behaving like some love-struck teenager!

Like some love-struck teenager. These words came out of Neha's mouth with giggles.

I wanted to give her a tight slap across her face. Nobody, nobody in the world, dares show such disrespect for me. I wanted her to know this, and I wanted to make sure that she would never ever do such a thing again. But Vineet interrupted me. I let him. Neha is a stupid woman, he said, looking straight into her eyes. Don't pay any attention to her. She watches too many films.

In one second that woman came crashing down to the ground. In my ears I heard the thud, and the truth is that I enjoyed hearing that sound. I should say here that I don't need another person, and I don't need a man, to fight my fights. I don't have parents, remember, and my husband is far away. Still, just like Vineet must have felt good fighting for me, I also felt good. The only problem now was that I looked at him in a different way. Now he was not just some sweet person who was always dressed in a nicely pressed shirt and pants. Now he was a man. Underneath those nice clothes there was a man's body.

⌒

But how do such small, little foolish thoughts matter? How does Vineet matter? What matters is that just now I cannot get sleep. I am frightened to close my eyes.

It is late at night now, that time in the night when the sky above is screaming with planes that bring people to their families, or sometimes take them away. The house is quiet, my son and my in-laws are sleeping peacefully, and I can't close my eyes. I can't close my eyes because as soon as they close my drunken son appears, howling, growling on his hands and knees, a mad dog vomiting and crawling around the bodies of two almost dying boys lying on the roadside. Each and every time I close my eyes I see Bobby crawling around his dying friends, a mad animal sniffing and scratching at their dirty, drunken bodies. And I don't know what to do.

Not such a long time ago, when my eyes closed for the night, a smart young man would be standing in front of me, a smart young man in a navy-blue suit that was stitched at the tailoring shop that Doctor Sahib goes to, the one in Connaught Place with an English name, Something & Sons, and this young man, my son Bobby, who looked like a young man in an advertisement for Raymond suits, was carrying not a briefcase but a slim laptop bag, in real leather, and his hair was cut short, and he was shaved and smart and clean, and standing straight, standing in front of me, his mother, and was saying bye-bye to me before he left for the office, which was located in one of those very modern new buildings in Gurgaon. This was what I would see night after night. This was the picture that would bring me peace and allow me three or four hours of sleep.

I know that I sound like just another mother gone mad with foolish fantasies about her son. But the truth is that my Bobby has everything that is required to be that picture. I don't like to boast, but the truth is that my Bobby has all the brains to get admission into an IIM for his MBA, and he is also six feet tall and has a handsome face, and his skin is so fair that in winter his cheeks glow pink. All that he has to do is forget about all those stupid cooking shows and recipe books, and apply himself a little bit more to his studies, and he has to stop slouching and fix his posture, and get his hair cut more regularly and shave at least one or two times a week. Then the whole world will see. That day he made a mistake, yes, but all young people make mistakes these days. But he also learnt his lesson, and I made very, very sure that he did, and one day, mark my words, one day my Bobby will be more than that man in the Raymond advertisement.

8

The anger was not going away. I tried my level best to push it to one side, to swallow it, to dissolve it in prayers, everything, but wherever I went it followed me. Wherever I went this anger followed me, pulling on my sari pallu like some needy child. The picture of my Bobby and the two dying boys was not going away. Each and every time I closed my eyes, each and every time I blinked, that picture appeared. I had to know what happened. I had to get my hands on the animal that sold that poison to three young boys, the animal that almost killed two young schoolboys and maybe almost killed my Bobby. I had to get my fingers around that animal's neck. But Bobby refused to tell me anything. All this time he has refused to say anything at all about that day. He has not even allowed me to meet the parents of the other boys. But I had to know. I had to come face to face with that animal. Then this morning, after begging him and threatening him for days and days, Bobby finally agreed to show me the shop from where they had bought the alcohol, but only if I allowed him to come with me. Obviously I had wanted to go alone. I did not want Bobby to see his mother be the animal that she had to be in front of another animal. But he would not listen, even though I tried my level best to convince him. That place is too dangerous, he kept saying. That place is too shady. You can't go there alone. So, I agreed to allow him to come with me.

It seems that evil lives closer to you than you would suspect it to. It seems that evil is even easier to buy than bananas. The shop from which Bobby and his friends bought the alcohol was closer to my house than the fruit seller that I go to every evening. And Bobby was right. It was well and truly a very shady place. From outside it looked like any workshop, a small, little shed filled with towers of old and new tyres, and there were small, little dirty boys loitering around. It looked like the type of place you went to to get a puncture repaired. But behind this shed was a small room, and I only call it a room because it had four walls and a ceiling, and as soon as I entered this small, dark and dirty room, or hole, or whatever you want to call it, as soon as I stepped into it, I wanted to vomit. I actually retched. There was the most horrible smell, a smell worse than anything that I had smelt before, a smell of kerosene and shit and chemicals all mixed together. And in every corner, on every shelf, there were packets and packets of what looked like powdered masalas, but were drugs, surely, packets and packets of them just sitting there openly on the shelves along with hundreds of bottles, small, little glass bottles, filled with a urine-coloured liquid that must have been the cheap country liquor that my Bobby had drunk. I quickly did some deep breathing. Then, in my strictest voice,

I told Bobby to wait outside, but he just stood behind me and refused to move. I looked up at a picture of Ganeshji above the door to steady myself.

I had thought that I would see a fat old man with a fat stomach in a vest and pyjamas, with henna-coloured hair and paan-stained teeth. That is what TV does to you. But instead of that what stood in front of me was a slim man who seemed to be about my husband's age, dressed in a baby pink shirt and grey pants, a balding man with metal-framed spectacles, who only had to wear a white coat to look like a lab technician in a doctor's office. I looked up at Ganeshji again, and then I turned to the man and spat on his face.

Bobby, who was standing behind me, caught my hand. I shook him off. And the man standing in front of me? He just took a folded white handkerchief out of the pocket of his pants, unfolded it, gently wiped my spit off his chin, folded it again and put it on the counter. Then he smiled.

Madamji, he said, looking not actually at me, but at some point behind me, at my son maybe. Madamji, what can I do for you?

I could not speak.

Madamji, you won't find what you are looking for over here.

I turned to Bobby, who looked like he was just going to cry, then I turned back to the man.

Madamji, he said, now looking up at Ganeshji's picture. Madamji, as a mother you pay not only for your own sins, but also for the sins of your child. And then he just left the room.

I tried my level best to stand steady, I closed my eyes and tried to do some deep breathing again, but all that I breathed in was that horrible, horrible smell of chemicals and shit. I turned again to Bobby. His eyes were now filled with tears.

When we walked out of the shop I felt the June sun attack my bones. It seemed that the anger that I had felt all these days had slowly burnt through my skin, burnt through my flesh, so that the June sun could attack my bare bones directly. Now, thirteen hours after the visit to that shop, my bones still feel that same heat.

⌒

As a mother you not only pay for your own sins, but you also pay for the sins of your child. How dare he say such things? How dare such an animal say such things? What does a criminal know about being a mother? What does a man know about being a mother? And what do they even mean, those stupid words? How can one person pay for the sins committed by another person? And why only the mother? Sharma Sahib, where are you? You were supposed to spend a month with us every year. Come back just now! Come back and take control of your son. Come back and pay for his sins. But what do you even know of your son's sins? Oh, my Bobby, you say. Oh, my poor Bobby. Oh, my sweet and studious Bobby. What do you know of your sinful son?

⌒

Many times when I am walking in the market or standing in a crowded train compartment, basically, whenever I am surrounded by a lot of people, I think about how each and every one of these people has or has had a mother, and then I think of all the hours, all the days and nights, all the years that are spent looking after children, and it seems that my head is going to burst. Such a lot of time! Such a lot of care! I wonder if anybody has ever bothered to think that if there are six billion people on this earth, and each and every one of them has a mother, dead or alive, what the total time spent would be on caring for others, on caring and compromise and sacrifice. I am sure that if anybody actually bothered to make such a calculation, that person's head would also burst.

Obviously there are those mothers who have easy lives. There are those mothers like my mother who were let off from their duties very early or mothers like Doctor Sahib's wife, modern maharanis, who have one ayah to feed their children, one ayah to clean their noses, one ayah to clean their shit, and what not. But then that is how the world is.

⌐

It is night-time. Papaji and Mummyji are sleeping in the hall, and Bobby is sleeping here in the corner on his cot, his headphones still in his ears, a cookbook resting on the pillow next to his cheek. You have to see this boy, this tall, beautiful boy. This man, almost. He would make any mother's heart burst with pride.

But what am I saying? Am I so stupid a woman that I could forget so quickly that this is the boy who betrayed his mother, who brought shame to her? Have I forgotten that this is the boy who drank?

It is night-time again, and again sleep will not come to me. Maybe now I have met the man who has blood on his hands. Maybe now I know the face of evil. I stood in front of it and spat on it. But then what? I still can't close my eyes. You won't find what you are looking for over here. That is what he said. And the truth is that what he said was right.

When I came back home from that man's shop I prayed. Except for preparing lunch and dinner, the only thing that I did today was pray. I prayed and I prayed and I prayed. I prayed until Mummyji came into the prayer room, and actually caught my shoulders and shook me, and asked me if I was fine. I prayed, but nothing. No answers, no peace, no peace that comes from answers. It seems that God was also saying one and the same thing to me. It seems that He was also saying, Madamji, you won't find what you are looking for over here.

But was it actually a sin that my Bobby committed? Is drinking such a sin? On Friday, when I met Doctor Sahib at the clinic, one thought came to me, the thought that if Doctor Sahib drinks alcohol, and I know that he does because his bearer had told me a long time ago about how his sahib drinks two glasses of whiskey every evening without fail and from time to time even the memsahib does, so if Doctor Sahib, who is such a respectable man, drinks, then why is it such a bad thing if my Bobby did? Should I have become so angry? Obviously Bobby is just a child, and he drank some cheap country liquor that almost killed him, not the imported whiskey that Doctor Sahib enjoys. Still, was it a sin or just a child's mistake?

God help me. What am I thinking?

⌒

I am not fine, Mummyji, I am not fine. Shake me up again. You are a mother, Mummyji. Only a mother can know the suffering of another mother. Help your daughter-in-law, Mummyji. She has gone mad. Tell your son to come back. You say that every boy has to have his father near him. Mummyji, every woman also has to have her husband near her.

9

Sometimes the goddess of night can be kind. Sometimes she will sit by your bed and rub away all those big and small fears that trouble you with the lamp-black of night-time, until they cannot be seen any more, so that maybe you can wake up strong the next morning.

Yesterday was a little bit difficult, I can't lie about that, but today has been much better. Except when I had a small fight on the phone with the mechanic who has still not come to fix the washing machine, and I have been calling him up daily for two weeks now, except for those two or three minutes in the morning, I have felt peaceful. Everything will be fine. I know it. Actually, I have always known it. Yesterday I behaved a little bit oddly, but it was only because I had temporarily forgotten this important fact. I think that you can forgive me. From time to time even people who are normally quite strong can feel that they have been beaten a little bit. Still, as I just said, it will all be fine. In less than two weeks my in-laws will leave for Canada for the birth of their grandchild, and they will only come back in October, which will give me enough time alone with Bobby to fix his life. And in only seventy-nine days' time my husband will be back in Delhi for his annual leave, and it will be just the three of us again. It will all be fine.

—

I have decided that I am going to buy Bobby a suit. I think that he has to have a suit, a smart two-piece suit. It will be good for him.

I have not gone mad. See, why is it that men wear suits to the office? Why is it a rule in government offices and big companies that all the employees have to dress properly? The reason is simple. The clothes that you wear every morning control how you think about yourself and how the world thinks about you. I have even seen this with myself. When I wear a smart, nicely starched sari to the clinic, I feel strong and important, I feel in control of all things and all people around me. I have even seen that the nurses, the cleaners, the lab assistants and technicians also give me a particular type of respect that I normally don't get when I am wearing a churidar kurta.

See, wearing a suit will help Bobby. Just now he is going through a difficult time, and the truth is that all teenagers go through these types of phases. But wearing a suit will give him a type of confidence that he does not have. Maybe it will also make him more disciplined. Not even ten or fifteen years ago, each and every school required boys to wear a blazer and tie as part of the school uniform. And how smart and confident the boys used to be. I remember so clearly seeing them waiting for their school buses on winter mornings, blazers and ties, shirts always tucked in properly, hair combed with a nice side parting. But that is all changing now. In my son's school, for example, the children now just wear these sweatshirts with hoods in winter, sweatshirts that are at least two sizes too big for them, with hoods. The smart blue blazer and striped tie are all gone. It is very sad to see today's schoolboys. The hair is never combed, the shirts are hanging out and their pants are so loose that half the time you can see their underwear. And are the girls any better? They shorten the hems of their skirts and roll their socks down to their ankles, and all around all you see are legs, naked legs. Don't school principals and all those important people in the Education ministry see how this affects children? Untidy dressing makes untidy minds. But I know that when my Bobby puts on the suit that I buy him, he will come to know something about what it feels like to be an important person, to be a powerful executive in a multinational company or an international bank.

Obviously I will have to lie to Bobby and tell him that I have bought the suit for a family wedding, because last year when I bought him a tie, he became very angry with me. I had bought it just like that, and that is the truth. I was walking around in Sarojini Nagar market, trying to buy socks for him, when I saw a beautiful silk tie with red paisleys in a showroom window, and it was on sale, and I thought that Bobby would look so handsome wearing it, and so I bought it. But what can I say? What is this? he shouted. No, he did not actually shout because Bobby is a good boy who does not raise his voice, especially not at his mother, but, What is this? he said, throwing the tie on the bed and looking at me like I had committed some big crime. Why did you buy this? What are you doing to me? What do you want from me? I was quite shocked by his reaction, but you know how boys of his age can be, and so I kept quiet. Still, my Bobby did wear it one time, in December, at my husband's cousin's wedding, and he looked even more handsome than I had imagined. Actually, he looked just like his father in the early days.

Maybe I should talk a little bit about my husband in his early days, about how handsome he was, how smart and handsome he was. It is not that my husband is not handsome now, but then, when he was younger, there was that special type of handsomeness, the boyish type of handsomeness that shines. I remember so clearly the first time I saw him. It was almost eighteen years ago, in December 1993. Still, I can see him so clearly in a light yellow shirt and navy-blue pleated pants, sitting on the divan in my father's house in Meerut, his hands fair and clean resting on his knees. He had come with his parents and sisters to meet me. And I remember how surprised I was that he was handsome. I knew that he would be a respectable boy, because my father would never ever have allowed him to put even one foot into our home if he was not a respectable boy hailing from a respectable family, but handsome? I did not expect any type of handsomeness. I had always thought that good looks and goodness don't come in the same package. I was wrong. Even our neighbour Jyoti Aunty used to tease me about how handsome my husband was. She thought that he looked like a film hero. So, when is Rajesh Khanna going to bless us with his presence again? she used to joke all the time.

The marriage offer had come some months before, through my husband's uncle who had a bakery next to my father's shop. Actually, my father received many offers for my hand. We never had a lot of money, but we were respectable, and I was also quite a pretty young girl, and so my father received many offers. But my father was not like most other fathers, he was not in any type of hurry to marry off his daughter. He was very particular about the type of boy that his daughter would marry. Even though he himself had a shop, he wanted me to marry a boy in service, not in business. My father was a very broadminded man and, for example, even though the boy obviously had to be Brahmin, the boy's subcaste did not matter very much to him. What was important to my father was that the boy be well educated and in a stable job, and hail from a good family. So, my father took his time to find out everything that he could about the Sharma family and their boy Dheeraj before allowing them to meet me.

I remember the scene so clearly, my husband sitting quietly on the divan between his mother and older sister, while our fathers sat on the two chairs in the corner near the TV. When I entered he looked up at me quickly, shyly, and then he looked down again at his hands. I sat down on the stool at one end of the divan, next to my mother-in-law, and spoke to her for some time about the weather, about the cost of vegetables and about my job. She said that she and her husband did not have a problem with girls working, even after marriage. I remember thinking that they were also broadminded, like my father. I remember feeling good, I remember feeling not scared.

After some time, after everybody had tea, my father told my husband and me to go to the veranda, so that we could have some time alone to come to know each other a little bit. Actually, my father had told me before the family came that he wanted me to spend a little bit of time alone with my prospective husband. That is how modern my father was. And you should have seen how shocked Poonam, my husband's older sister, was. It was very, very funny. She almost choked on her biscuit. She is actually quite traditional, more traditional than her parents, I think. When we were going on our honeymoon, for example, she even checked my suitcase to make sure that I did not pack any indecent clothes. But at least she did not accompany us on our honeymoon, as my friend's sister-in-law did. So, we went to the veranda, my prospective husband and I, and we sat down on the two new pink plastic chairs that my father had especially bought for that meeting.

What do you think? is the first thing my husband said to me.

About what? I said, even though I knew what he was talking about.

About me, he said.

You are not as tall as I thought you would be, I said.

He was quiet for some time, and then he said, I can be as tall as you want me to be.

And when he said that I knew that this was the boy I was going to marry.

It is as clear as a photo, it seems that I am holding the photo in my hands just now, a photo of my husband and me sitting in my father's veranda. I am wearing my mother's red and gold Benarsi silk sari, and he is sitting next to me, in his yellow shirt and blue pants, and with his knees together he is leaning just a little bit to his left, into me. It is quite a nice photo, actually. It almost looks like a poster from some romantic film.

But let me not speak any more about my handsome husband and other foolish things. So, yes, now I have to buy my Bobby a suit. This weekend I will go to buy my Bobby a smart two-piece suit, because three-piece suits are well and truly out of fashion now, and I will buy it readymade from one of the showrooms on the ground floor of Select Citywalk. I know it will be much costlier than getting it tailored here in Malviya Nagar, but it does not matter. My husband works in Dubai. From time to time things like this have to be allowed.

10

Vineet and I were at the mall looking at computers because I had thought that before I tell Doctor Sahib which model I want I should actually see and touch some real machines rather than just look at photos on the Internet, so we were at this huge electronics showroom, Vineet and I, when suddenly, just like that, Vineet said, How is your brother?

For five or six seconds I just stood there, staring at him. I could not understand what he was trying to ask me.

Don't worry, he said. I know that your brother was sick.

I remained quiet.

I also know that you don't want to tell me about it, he said. But I just want you to know that I know and that I can help you if you want me to help you.

I tried to steady myself, then I tried to laugh, and then I said, You did not tell me that you were also a doctor, Mr F&B.

What else could I say? While standing there in the middle of a showroom in the mall I could not have burst into tears and said, Sorry, Vineetji, for lying to you for such a long time, but that boy, that boy you saw is not my brother, he is my son. I could not have said, Vineetji, I have a son and he was not just sick, but he was poisoned, poisoned by some cheap country liquor, and now that you know that I have a son, you now also know that I have a husband, and while my husband works like a donkey in Dubai, I loiter around at a mall with you. You, some man I met on the Metro. I could not have said this, and why should I have said this anyway? Vineet is nobody to me, and I am nobody to him. We are two people who met each other on the Metro by chance, and from time to time we talk on the train or go out together, and that is all. He knows nothing about me, he has never ever bothered to ask, and so I don't have to tell him anything.

But I did ask him how he knew that I had a brother, and when I did he turned his head away, to his left shoulder, then he muttered something.

I can't hear you, I said.

I saw you at the station, he said quietly.

What? I said

I had just got off the train, he said. This was around two weeks ago, in the evening, and I was walking to the escalator when I saw you and your brother get off the other train.

So? I said. So what? I was so angry that I was almost shouting.

You were carrying a big envelope, which had Safdarjang Hospital printed in big letters, and you were holding your brother's hand. You did not see me.

Congratulations, Inspector Sahib, I said.

Your brother looked so weak, he said.

How does it matter to you? I said.

I wanted to come up to you, he said. You looked so tired and I wanted to help you, but I did not want to embarrass you.

When he said this something inside me melted. In some place between my chest and my stomach some hard thing inside me melted. And I think that if anybody at all had seen his eyes, small and so kind, I swear on God that they were very much like the eyes of Shirdi Sai Baba, if anybody at all had seen his eyes as he talked to me, something inside that person would also have surely melted. So then I told Vineet to forget about all this and I suggested to him that we look for a suit for my brother. It will cheer him up, I said. I said, After all that my brother has suffered, I think that a nice two-piece suit will cheer him up.

⌒

There were one or two minutes at the showroom, while Vineet and I were talking about my so-called brother, when I had, I don't know how, stepped out of this small, little drama between us and I was standing on one side, just watching two people, a young man in a red collared t-shirt and blue jeans, a good looking man, I can't lie, and hardly one foot in front of him an older woman, a thirty-seven-year-old woman in an orange chanderi sari, her long hair in a loose bun, quite pretty but a little bit plump, but then what type of man wants a woman who has bones sticking out from every place? From outside this small, little drama it was a nice photo of a handsome couple, and I think that anybody who saw us would have thought the same.

Still, that is not how it is from inside. Maybe we are handsome together, Vineet and I, but we are not a couple. I am very clear about that and I thought that he was also clear about it, until this afternoon. Now I wonder. If he thinks that I have a teenage brother, then how old does he actually think that I am? Twenty? And if he thinks that I am so young, then how does he actually see me? Does he actually think that the two of us together make a pair? How does he feel?

I have never lied to him. I have never ever tried to make him see me as anybody other than the person that I am, and if there are some things that he does not know about me, it is only because he has never bothered to ask me or he has shut my mouth up if I have tried to tell him. What did he tell me that day at his stupid hotel? I don't want to know anything. Isn't that what he said? I don't need to know anything about you, a person is not supposed to ask for more than what is given to him, and what not. Has he forgotten all that? Whatever it is, whatever it is that he thinks and wants, Vineet better understand fast, he better understand once and for all, that I am a good woman, a respectable woman, and my mind is clear, and also my heart, and they are in the right places, with my family and my home, and I am not interested in anything but friendship, the type of friendship shared between two women. The truth is that he could have just been a Vineeta to me. Man or woman, it would not make any difference, and that is the truth.

So, let Vineet think what he wants to think, let him want what he wants. But I am not going to waste any more time on such foolish things. I know myself, I am clear about what I feel, and just now I have more important things to do. My in-laws are leaving on Friday. There is a lot of shopping to be done and I also have to help them pack, and then after they are gone, I have to do the most important thing of all. I have to fix Bobby. My in-laws are good people, they are good people and try their level best to be as helpful as they can, but from time to time they interfere. It is already so difficult trying to discipline a fifteen-year-old boy, and, actually, he will be sixteen years of age in less than four months, but with grandparents around, it makes it much, much more difficult. Oh ho, you are so strict with Bobby, they say to me. Or, Poor Bobby, he is only a child. And what not. But they will be gone in less than one week, and they will be gone for more than three months, and Vineetji, I can't keep wasting my time loitering around with you at malls. I am a mother. I have much more important things to do. I have to use this time to bring up my son properly, as a mother has to do, as a mother only can.

11

There is nothing in the whole world as nice as riding in an auto in the rain. The air is cool, the sky is the colour of grey pearls, the trees are clean, clean and green, and nothing, not one bad thought, not even the auto's side flap, can keep the happiness of the pre-monsoon away. What a nice time we had yesterday, my Bobby and I. Even though it was Sunday, it was so nice. It was probably the best Sunday in the nineteen months since my husband left us. The morning, obviously, was spent at home. Bobby completed his holiday homework, because his school opens in just two weeks, and I cleaned the prayer room and opened out the hems of Bobby's school pants. And because my in-laws have left for Canada, I also put away their folding cots. But afterwards, my Bobby and I went for an outing.

The truth is that I wanted to see my son smile. I wanted to see his eyebrows jump halfway up his forehead and his eyes shine as he smiled. And so I suggested to him that we dress up nicely and go to the mall to watch a film and eat dinner in a restaurant. Bobby shaved, and he wore a smart collared t-shirt and clean jeans. I think that Bobby also likes to make his mother smile.

The film we watched was just some mindless comedy about four stupid robbers, but the seats in the hall were covered in some type of soft, beautiful red velvet and the air-conditioning was so good that I just rested my head on Bobby's shoulder and had the most peaceful sleep of my life.

After the film we went to the food court for dinner. We actually don't go out to eat these days because my in-laws think that restaurant food is too oily and costly, and that most of it can be made at home anyway, but I think, and I don't want to disrespect my in-laws, but I think that from time to time everybody needs to have a change, everybody needs to have a little bit of fun. And my husband also always thought that. When he was here we would go out to eat each and every weekend without fail.

The food court is something to be seen. I have come to this mall many times, but I have never actually eaten at the food court. And what a nice place it is! Even though there were hundreds and hundreds of people, it was all so properly organised, everybody standing in lines at the food counters, everybody waiting so patiently for their orders. And to have so many different types of food in one place! There was Chinese and South Indian and Italian, and there was American, obviously, and then tandoori items and parathas, and what not. All in one place. It actually took us almost half an hour to decide what we wanted to eat.

We talked a lot, my Bobby and I. Obviously we first talked about the dishes we were eating, because that is what Bobby likes to talk about. So, we talked about all the whole masalas and powdered spices that would have been used in them, the types of utensils that they were cooked in, whether they were cooked on high or low flame, and what not. Then we talked about my husband. I told Bobby about what a good father my husband is, what a good husband he is to me, because from time to time I think that it is important to say such things to one's children, and I told him how I am sure that one day Bobby himself will also be like that. I also told him, and I asked him to listen to me very carefully while I talked, that we will never ever be a burden on him, that we will never ever ask him for even one rupee, and that that is one of the main reasons why his father is away from us in Dubai. Then I told him about my future business plans, about how I plan to start a training institute or academy for office management, where youngsters will learn to use the latest word-processing and spreadsheet software on the latest computers, where they will learn Business English and how to conduct themselves in job interviews. I said that I plan to open the business after eight or ten years, after my husband comes back from Dubai, and that I plan to rent a place for it in Begumpur, since Malviya Nagar and Shivalik have become too costly.

I asked Bobby what he thought of all this. He was quiet for some time, his eyes were fixed on his plate, so I asked him again.

Ma, you are always planning, he said, with his head still bent over his plate.

So what is wrong with that? I said.

Nothing, he said quietly.

So then? I said. Everybody plans. Do you know that even a man like Doctor Sahib plans for his retirement? All these people keep coming to meet him from different banks, selling him life insurance policies and ULIPs and SIPs and what not. It is financial planning. Planning. That is why he is so rich.

Now Bobby lifted his head up and rested his eyes on my eyes. Ma, he said, those people have to plan, but people like us don't have to.

What do you mean? I said.

They have many more years to live than we have.

Stop talking such nonsense, I said.

But now he kept talking. Look at how you work, he said. Day and night, at home, at the clinic. Work, work, work. And Papa also. Double-shifts in the hospital, hardly eating, working, working, working.

Everybody has to work, I said. Your grandfather always used to say that great things can only be achieved with great effort.

What great things, Ma? Bobby said. And are your bodies supposed to pay such a great price for it? You are thirty-seven years of age now, no? And Papa is how old? Forty? Forty-one? After all the work that you both have done, do you actually think that your poor bodies will survive long enough to enjoy these great things?

The truth is that for one second I wanted to cry. Forgetting, just for that one second, that he is only a child and that children always say all types of foolish things, forgetting all this I wanted to run to the washroom to cry. But I did some deep breathing as fast as I could, and then I laughed and I said, You want to kill off your poor parents so quickly?

Now, obviously, I realise, after one long day, that it was foolish of me to talk to Bobby about such things, and it was even more foolish of me to ask him for his thoughts. This is not how you treat your child. You should not allow him entry into your world by talking about grown up topics. And the future is a grown up topic, just like money is a grown up topic. They are complicated ideas. To enter into the world of grown ups, to understand the complicated ideas that make this world, you first have to have the mind of a grown up. If you bring a child into a grown up's world, you will surely disturb his unprepared mind. What is the future for a child? It is one hour from the present. What is money for a child? The latest phone. This is different from our ideas about the future, our ideas about money. So why talk about such things with our children? Why trouble them? Just like you have to study and take exams to qualify for a job, you have to take some tests and do some training to prepare for the world of grown ups. We should wait for them to be prepared. And we also should not rush them into such preparations. As it is a child has such a short time in his child's world. Why not let him enjoy that short, trouble-free time?

I will not make such a mistake again.

Another thing happened there at the mall. While we were eating, I suddenly saw Mrs Khanna, Mrs Something Khanna. I have forgotten her name but I have it in my files. She was Doctor Sahib's patient for many years. Mrs Khanna was there at the food court, sitting just three or four tables away from us, with three ladies, all of them dressed in long blouses and those odd capri pants that seem to be in fashion these days, the ones that stop, just like that, somewhere halfway down the lower legs, as if all the cloth at the factory had got finished. So, she was there with her friends, all skinny ladies with fat bags, all of them with their hair dyed in a foreigner-brown colour, and I have to say that I sometimes wonder how these type of people spend such a lot of money on their hair, on the clothes that they wear, only to look like a photocopy of the person sitting next to them, so, she was sitting there with her photocopies when she also saw me, and then she smiled. Mrs Khanna actually smiled. She raised her hand up a little bit, waved and smiled at me.

She looked so old. She could not have been more than forty-four or forty-five years of age, but if you saw her you would have surely thought that she was sixty years of age. Her face was covered in fancy cosmetics, her hair was dyed in a goldeny-brown colour and her body was as slim as a film star's, but all that did not matter. Mrs Khanna looked older than my mother-in-law. She looked so bad that I actually felt sad. I smiled back at her.

I remember her case clearly because she came to the clinic for so many years. The problem was that she could not have a child. Week after week she came, even her husband came, and they did test after test and every type of procedure, and rounds and rounds of IVF, but even a big doctor like Doctor Sahib could not grant her a child. I think that it was for six or seven years that she tried before she finally gave up. And now here she was, a woman ageing without a child.

Before I started working at the clinic I don't think that I had actually ever met any woman, any grown up woman, without a child. I am sure that they were there in Meerut, but I had not actually ever thought about this idea until I started working at the clinic, this idea of a childless woman. Now, when I see these ladies lining up one after another at the clinic, I wonder sometimes what it means to not be a mother. I wonder how it feels to not have to carry the weight of another life for each and every second that God grants you on this earth. Does it feel good or bad? Do you fly freely without any worry in the world or do you just float around without any purpose at all? Most of the time I feel sorry for such women who will never feel that special type of happiness that only a mother can feel, who will never feel that special type of pride in a child that only a mother can feel, feel deep in the womb that held her child long ago. Still, the truth is, and I don't want to be ungrateful, and I feel well and truly blessed that I was granted such a beautiful boy, but the truth is that from time to time I also feel jealous. Even if you are just floating here and there without any purpose, at least you are not pulled down by the weight of your child.

So, when I saw Mrs Khanna, when I saw her ageing face ageing very much before it was time for it to age, I wondered what had made her so old. If she had no children, who had drawn those lines on her face?

⌒

But why speak of such things any more? Why not let the lovely wet wind blow away such thoughts? You have to see the peepul tree outside. Its leaves are silver now in the rainy wet light. It seems that this pre-monsoon rain has come from God. It has come to bless me before I start my work on fixing Bobby. Now that my in-laws are gone, I have to start my work immediately.

⟶

My in-laws left the day before yesterday. Our neighbour's son Kamal works in a travel agency that has contacts at the RPO, so we had no problems in making their passports. Kamal is a good person to know. One day I will also have to get a passport to go abroad. I will travel in a plane. Maybe I will go to Dubai to meet my husband. But then he says that it hardly feels like a foreign place. He says that even though there are some white people here and there, it actually just feels like some fancier type of India, an India that has been cleaned up nicely. And, obviously, it also does not snow there. So, what is the use in spending such a lot of money to go to such a place? Instead of Dubai, maybe we should go to Switzerland. Or maybe we should wait a little bit more, until Bobby is happily settled in America or England, and go to meet our son. Yes, we will go to meet our son in America or England, we will go to meet our son and his family, and Bobby will bring our grandchildren to the airport to pick us up, and then he will drive us back to his beautiful house in his big SUV, and our daughter-in-law will have a hot and tasty meal prepared for us after our long plane journey, and after we have eaten, after we have sat down and eaten and exchanged all the news, after that I will go out into Bobby's garden and play with my grandchildren in the snow.

Yes, that is where we will go. But before Bobby's parents can make that journey, Bobby has to make another type of journey first. Maybe it will be a little bit long and a little bit difficult, but with his mother by his side he will, by God's grace, surely make it.

12

Last evening Vineet smsed me to call him up. Actually, he sent me six smses to call him up before I finally picked up the phone. The reason that I took such a long time to call him up is because I thought that I was confused. Ever since that day when we met each other at the electronics showroom, which was two weeks ago, I had been feeling a little bit odd, and I had thought that this feeling was confusion, and I don't like to feel confused because confusion is actually a sickness, a sickness suffered by the weak-minded, and I don't like to boast, but I am not a weak-minded person normally, I am actually a person who has quite a lot of strength, which, I think, was a gift from my father, an inheritance, an inheritance that I want to pass down to my son. So, I did not want to keep feeling confused and that is why I did not want to talk to Vineet. But then after thinking about this for some time I realised that I have not actually been confused. What I have suffered is not actually the disease of confusion, but just the headache of two or three unanswered questions. And so I called him back.

See, all of us live with questions that cannot be answered. As long as we can answer our own questions with honesty, we should not worry about those questions that only others have answers for but sometimes refuse to share with us. That is how it is, and so not only did I call him up, but I also agreed to meet him when he asked me if I was free this morning.

And what did Vineet want? He just wanted me to go with him today to see some new properties in Greater Noida. The MCD, he said, had issued his mother a show cause notice for the illegal construction of a second room in their flat, and they were always harassing them and asking them for money, and his mother's blood pressure was always so high because of this, and so she told Vineet that he had to get them out of that place immediately, before the MCD killed her, and because an order from his mother is like an order from God, this is what Vineet himself said, he needed my help, he needed a woman's ideas, to buy a new house.

It was a very interesting experience, and more importantly, it was very educational. We went to six different properties in Greater Noida and Noida Extension, and what can I say? Each one was better than the other. One had Italian marble in the drawing and dining rooms, and we thought that it was so beautiful, but then the next one had one of those new modular kitchens with all the latest appliances. One had false ceilings with fancy lights, but then the other had imported cupboards and what they called Velvet Touch Paints and Textures. It was so difficult to choose. And even though all the buildings were still under construction, the developers had made these beautiful show flats so that prospective buyers could see what they would finally look like. This was my favourite part. It was so nice to walk through the flats, to walk around all the different, different rooms, to sit on a beautiful sofa, to stand in front of a shining gas stove. Maybe it looked like a film studio, because there was not even one stain or scratch on the walls, and the floors were shining, and there was all this beautiful Italian furniture that was so nicely arranged. Maybe it looked a little bit artificial, but still, it all seemed very real to me. I imagined myself in these flats. In each show flat that we saw, I imagined my husband and I living there retired and happy, our Bobby well settled in a foreign country, and the two of us here, with respectable neighbours all around us, neighbours who had beautiful dogs that they took for morning walks, neighbours whose children were also working abroad. It was so easy to imagine all this and my husband and I growing old together in a nice, new, modern flat.

But obviously the purpose of this outing was to find a suitable flat for Vineet and his mother, not for me to build dreams from dream houses, and so at each property I would think about all its advantages and disadvantages, always keeping in mind the needs of these two people. At each property, Vineet and I would not only spend time at the show flat, but we would walk around the whole complex with the agent and ask him questions about power back-up and water supply, facilities offered, malls and hospitals nearby, and what not. Then after we would finish, Vineet would turn to me and ask me for my comments, which I would think about carefully before saying. And I think that he thought that my comments were quite useful.

After looking at properties, Vineet suggested that we go to eat Chinese food at a restaurant in the Sector 18 market in Noida. I agreed, and the food was very tasty. But then suddenly, in the middle of eating, he again asked me about my so-called brother. Obviously I was a little bit shocked. I was even a little bit angry that he had brought up this topic again. But then I realised that it was understandable that he did. Bobby was just a walking skeleton when Vineet saw us at the station, he was just a set of bones holding on to its mother. So, I decided to answer him properly this time. And when I started talking, I just could not stop. I blabbered on and on about the sad little story of my sick little brother, I told him about all the little, little things that had happened, I told him about how difficult everything was, and I don't know for how long I talked. I just could not stop. It was very odd behaviour. I never ever talk about my son like that to anybody. Actually, is there any parent who would? So why did I talk like this today? And with Vineet? I have spent some time this evening thinking about this and I think that I finally have an answer. I talked freely about Bobby's problems because I was talking about my so-called brother, not my son. I talked freely because it is much easier to talk about a troubled brother than to talk about a troubled child. I talked freely because my troubled brother's troubles are not my fault.

So, at this Chinese restaurant I talked and talked about Bobby, and Vineet listened with those same small, serious eyes fixed steadily on my eyes, and then just when we were going to finish our food, he gave me this odd type of look, this look where his eyes suddenly became bright and scared at the same time, and then, just like that, he reached over the table and put his hand on my arm.

I allowed it to rest there, Vineet's hand. It was a warm, heavy hand, it was the hand of a man. It was not even two centimetres bigger than my hand, but it had much more weight. I know that this sounds almost funny, but as it rested there, this hand on my arm, I suddenly remembered the first time that my husband had laid his body down on me. I remembered how I had thought, during those moments, that even though my husband was slim and hardly one inch taller than me, he was much, much heavier than me, and I remembered how I had then said to myself, while my husband's body was still on top of me, I had said to myself, Renu, this is what it is. All this love and romance and everything that happens between a man and a woman? This is what it is. It is the greater density of a man's bones, the greater weight of him that will give to his woman both peace and pain.

The truth is that for that one minute I wanted to take Vineet's hand, that hand that lay on my arm, and I wanted to put it on another part of my body. But I got up. I got up so suddenly that my chair fell back. Vineet also jumped up. Then I told him that it was getting late and I had to go back home now. He muttered something that I could not understand and we left.

⌒

When I reached home it was two o'clock and I could not believe it but my Bobby had prepared lunch, a poori–aloo lunch, for both of us. What was a bigger surprise was how clean the kitchen was. I had to pretend that I had not eaten already so I quickly sat down at the dining table, and as I took my first bite, Bobby stood in front of me patiently, waiting for my reaction.

This is so tasty, I said, and I actually was not lying.

You are just saying that to make me happy, he said.

Not at all, I said. It is the best poori-aloo I have ever eaten.

Better than Dadima's? he said.

Better than Dadima's, I said.

Then I am going to cook for you daily, he said.

I did not say anything. He looked so happy that I actually did not want to spoil his mood. And so he brought me one hot poori after another and refused to eat himself until I was finished.

I spent the rest of today as I normally spend every Saturday, changing bed sheets, grinding masalas, going to the market, and what not, but I did not feel as I normally do. Even Bobby, being such a sensitive boy, felt that something was wrong with his mother and kept asking me if I was fine. I told him that I had eaten too many pooris and so my stomach was feeling a little bit bloated. Obviously I was lying. But what could I have said to my son? Could I have told him that it was not overeating that troubled me but actually the opposite of that, some type of hunger?

As soon as Bobby went to sleep I sent an sms to my husband to call me up. I needed to hear the sound of my husband, my ears needed to hear the sound of those soft, low tones that, depending on my mood, can soothe me like songs of love or God, or excite me.

When he called me up we talked about various things. We talked about his boss and my boss, we talked about Bobby, and I also told him about how I have been trying to call up the mechanic to come to fix the washing machine. And then I said, Do you miss my body?

For two or three seconds he was quiet, then he said, You have become a very bold woman since I left, no?

Never mind all that, I said. Tell me now, do you still want my body?

Obviously I do, you fool, he said.

And I knew that he was not lying. His voice could not hide his hunger for me. My husband has always wanted my body. Then I asked him how he lived without sex and he said that it was very difficult and that the other men he lives with, all four of them, go to this one nurse, an Anglo-Indian Christian, who works at the hospital in the radiology department.

I don't care about those men, I said. What about you?

You have become a very bold woman, no? he said again. And then he finally told me how he masturbates while thinking about me, and that sometimes it is so bad, sometimes he misses my body such a lot, that he has to masturbate in the hospital bathroom during working hours.

My husband did not ask me if I also miss his body, if I miss two warm, heavy hands moving over my body. Did he feel too shy to ask? Or does he think that women don't suffer those types of hunger? Whatever it is, my husband will come to know the answers soon. In two months' time, exactly fifty-nine days from today on 31 August 2011, he will be here in Delhi, and when his son is in a deep sleep at night-time and the washing machine has started, my husband will come to know the answers.

13

There are days when the smallest, simplest things that you normally do every day without even knowing that you are doing them suddenly seem so difficult, days when a small, little thing like boiling milk seems more difficult than climbing a mountain. This morning my bones felt heavy like stone. And also my mind. And what was the crime for such a punishment? I asked Bobby to try on a suit. That is all. A suit. Bobby, see, I bought you such a smart suit! I said. And what did he do?

Ma! he said, almost shouting. What are you doing to me?

What am I doing to you? I said. I am asking you to try on a suit. A suit, that is all.

I don't want to wear a suit! he said.

I told him how it was not just any suit, that it was bought from the mall. Still, did he listen?

What are you trying to make me into? he said. I don't want to wear a suit! I don't want to do an MBA! I don't want to work in an office!

I am not trying to make you anything, you foolish boy, I said. I am only asking you to try on a suit that I bought especially for you with such a lot of love.

Still, did he listen? I don't want this, I don't want that, he went on and on, and then suddenly he said, I don't want to go to school any more.

I could not believe what I was hearing. He does not want to go to school? Children can be so foolish and difficult sometimes.

So, first I tried my level best to talk to him with love. I tried to tell him how important education is, how as Bobby's grandfather used to say, Knowledge is a treasure that no thief can touch. And do you know what he said? He said that he agreed that education is important but that he wanted to get his education at his friend Ankit's father's restaurant, and not at school, which he said was timewaste.

You want to be a cook? I said.

Not a cook, Ma, he said. I want to be a chef.

And do what? I said. Chop onions in some small dirty restaurant-kitchen in Saket?

But then I did some deep breathing and tried to explain to him nicely that people like us don't do such things, that maybe cooking is fine as timepass, but that it is not a suitable career for our type of people. I reminded him that he hails from a family that believes that education, a proper education, is more important than anything else in the world. I told him how even when my mother was dying my father made me attend school each and every day. I told him how my grandmother, his great grandmother, was dressed up as a boy, how her hair was cut short and her chest was pressed flat with a dupatta, just so that she could go to the only school in the village, which was a boys' school.

Bobby kept quiet. I could see that he was a little bit agitated and angry, so I decided to let it be. I also realised that I was getting angry for no reason, because Bobby is just a child, and this is just a phase, and he will quickly forget about all this leaving school and cooking business, and come back to normal.

⟜

It is a quarter to twelve at night. After surfing the Net and looking at some more computer models to see which one Doctor Sahib should buy for me, I am now lying in my bed. Bobby is sleeping on the folding cot. From the way his body is lying heavy and still, from the way his arm is hanging off his cot, it seems that by God's grace he is peaceful now, even if his mother is not.

I am tired. I wish I could go away. Sometimes I think that Bobby also wishes his mother would go away. Sometimes, like this morning, it seems that his eyes are saying to me, Ma, I wish that you had gone to Dubai instead of Papa. The truth is that from time to time I also wish that.

And so what if I did go away? Would something so horrible actually happen? Maybe we are all like those lizards in my husband's favourite little story, and maybe like those lizards we all give ourselves more importance than we actually deserve. So what if I am my son's mother? Does that mean that if I step away the world will come crashing down on him? He will still live, he will still grow. And I have to know this better than anybody else. My own mother died when I was fourteen years of age. And I think that I am fine. I am fine because whenever I have needed a mother, God has always brought me some very kind woman as a replacement. At school there was Sister Monica who told me about periods and bras and what not. When I was getting married, it was Nirmal Bua, my father's cousin-sister, accompanied by her two daughters, who did all the wedding preparations, all the cooking, getting me ready, everything. And when Bobby was born, it was my dear mother-in-law. How lovingly my mother-in-law treated me. Obviously she took great care of Bobby, he was her first and only grandson, but I cannot forget how she also took care of me. Day in and day out she cooked the types of food a new mother needs to have, and she massaged my back, massaged my legs, and took Bobby from me so that I could get sleep. All these women, at different times of my life, were mothers to me.

But why am I saying all this? I am not going anywhere and by God's grace I have good health and I will live long and there will be no need for God or anybody else to find a replacement for me in my son's life. But I think that what I want to say is that just because I am a mother, it does not mean that I can perform miracles. I can try my best to keep Bobby on the straight road because, as my father used to say, Nobody ever gets lost on the straight road, and I will say that I have always tried my best to do that from the first second that my son was born and I will keep trying until the day I die. But I am not God. I will never ever stop trying to do everything that I can do to make sure that my Bobby grows up to be a happy, healthy, successful man, but finally it is all in God's hands. Finally, He will decide my son's fate. And surely God would not want Bobby to be a cook. So, why should I actually worry such a lot?

⌒

From time to time I miss my husband. On a night when I feel like this I miss my husband very much. I want him to be here. I want him to start the washing machine and take off his clothes quickly, then take off my clothes, then I want him to do what a husband is supposed to do, as he used to do when he was here. And when all that is finished, when our bodies have become hot and our hearts have become happy, I want him to wash himself and wear his night suit and lie down next to me and close his eyes and go to sleep quickly, so that I can then talk to him, his sleeping body, a sleeping body that listens quietly, that listens without giving more words, as I used to do when he was here.

14

Then there are days when you could tell me to run all the way up to Vaishno Devi and down again, and I would be able to do it without any effort at all. I would be able to do it carrying an elephant on my back. Today I feel lighter again, but strong. I can move. That stone-heavy feeling has lifted. Now I actually feel warm blood flowing freely through my body. I feel good, finally. I feel well and truly good and strong again. I think that I could float.

I met Vineet on Thursday, his off-day, and it was nice. He invited me to his house, and because Bobby was going to Nehru Place after school with his friend Ankit, I agreed. And I don't think that it was wrong.

Do you want to come to my house? he had said on Monday morning when we were on the train.

Your house? I said.

Yes, my house.

I did not say anything.

Then he said, My house is just a house, it is not some disco bar.

And your mother? I said.

She has gone out of station, he said.

And so I went.

And what did we do? Most of the time we only talked. We talked about many topics, like the bomb blasts in Mumbai the evening before, his mother, hill stations. I like to talk to him. He does not talk too much, he never talks without reason, but when he speaks, he speaks intelligently, whether it is about the problems with Muslims or about women's minds or about the Himalayas. And he did ask me about Bobby again, How is your brother? he said, and I did not mind. I told him about how Bobby wanted to leave school, how he wanted to be a cook of all things, and that nobody at home could understand what to do. But this time, after listening to me quietly for quite a long time, Vineet actually offered me advice, which he had never ever done before.

Maybe your parents should not force him, he said to me. Maybe they should make him understand it for himself.

You know a lot about all this, I said jokily. How many children are you hiding from me?

He laughed, and then he said, Do you remember that TV serial *Fauji*?

I did remember it. My father used to go to the neighbour's house to watch it. The Shahrukh Khan serial, no? I said.

Yes, but at that time nobody knew him, Vineet said.

So? I said. You wanted to be a soldier?

I think that I was only seven or eight years of age when it started, he said. But, you know, I watched each and every episode, even during my exams. It used to come on Wednesdays. I never ever missed it. I wanted to be a commando. Even after the serial ended, for years and years that was my only dream. To be a commando. But my parents were totally against it. How can we give our only child to the army? they used to say. How can we let our son die? For years and years my father shouted at me and my mother cried, but I refused to listen. Then one day when I was in the eleventh standard my father enrolled me in the NCC and I was sent for one of those training camps.

And you couldn't eat the food? I said.

And I couldn't shit in a mud-hole, he said.

We both laughed, and I understood what he was trying to tell me.

See, this is the type of person Vineet is. When he says something to you, there is a proper reason for it. There is some lesson. That is why I like to talk to him.

After we talked for some time I told him that it was getting late and that we should eat our lunch. What can I say? He had cooked for me. There were eight dishes, I think, all from different parts of the world. He had made baked vegetables, pasta in red sauce, Chinese noodles that was nothing like the chowmein we normally eat, but something so tasty, with mushrooms and broccoli, and then paneer and dal and vegetable biryani and salad. Nobody has ever cooked for me like this before. And so we spent the rest of the afternoon just eating and talking. We ate all this tasty food and then we just talked, and that is all.

⌐

When I came back home from Vineet's house I decided to make an agreement with Bobby. I told him that as long as he gets good marks in class and comes back home by seven o'clock and studies properly at night-time, he could go and work in Ankit's father's restaurant two days a week after school. I also made him promise me that he would take no money, not one paisa, from Ankit's father, because as soon as somebody gives you money, no matter what the reason for it is and no matter how big or small the amount is, that person, that person who pays you, will now have power over you, will now be able to control you. I set these conditions and Bobby agreed to them happily.

I know that this was probably a foolish thing, but what could I do? Day in and day out Bobby had been lying around the house with a long face, telling me how he hates school and how he wants to be a chef. My hands were tied. And the truth is that I don't want to be like those other mothers who discipline their children with a stick. So, I thought that if I let him go to that restaurant he will very quickly understand for himself how foolish he is to get into all this cooking business.

I should thank Vineet for this. I should thank him for this clearness of mind and lightness of body. But is it only men who can do this? Why is it that when I come out of the prayer room or walk out of a temple I don't feel this clearness, this lightness? Is it only men who have the words and actions that make a woman feel fine? Is it only men who have that magic?

The nuns at the convent school used to tell us that God did not speak for four hundred years. But that was their God. Let those Christians wait another four hundred years for their one and only great God to speak to them. But what about You, Durga Ma? You can't just quietly stand there draped in pretty cloths and pretty flowers and pretty scents. Speak to me, my Durga Ma. Come to me. Don't make me go to men.

15

Now I know why Durga Ma behaves the way that She does. Now I know why She is always quiet. It is not because she is God. No. It is because She is a woman, and only a woman understands that life is complicated and that life's problems cannot be solved with ten or twenty simple words. But if you tell a man your troubles, he just quickly throws a solution to you, and because you are hungry and desperate for it you quickly swallow it up, like a desperate and hungry dog you swallow it up. And then what happens?

I told Vineet about how Bobby wanted to be a cook, he told me what to do, I listened to him, and you know what happened? I smelt alcohol. This evening, when Bobby came back from the restaurant, I swear on God, I swear on my husband, that I could smell alcohol. I was not born yesterday. I know that smell, that too sweet smell that attacks your head and your stomach, and makes you want to vomit. And I am sure that this was the smell that Bobby brought back home today. Even now, as that boy sleeps here on his cot, I can smell it.

What a fool I have been, what a stupid, stupid fool. I thought that everything was fine. Since my in-laws left, Bobby and I, the two of us by ourselves, have been spending a lot of time together, and after I allowed Bobby to work at the restaurant, he has been in such a good mood, and we have been talking and laughing such a lot together. And the truth is that for all these weeks I had actually removed from my mind that time in June when Bobby went to hospital. I had told myself that after the type of scolding I gave him he would never ever do such a thing again, and then I forgot the matter, totally forgot it, because difficult times have to be forgotten, they have to be left behind in their place in the past so that we can move forward.

What a fool I have been. What a fool I was to listen to Vineet.

⌒

Men like Doctor Sahib drink alcohol, but they are different to our men. They drink for different reasons. Men like Doctor Sahib drink because they are happy, not to become happy. Drinking for them is timepass, enjoyable timepass, like watching a film or eating in a nice restaurant. They drink to celebrate their life, not to escape it. You come to know this just by seeing how they drink. Doctor Sahib and his type of people sit in their own houses in beautiful rooms on soft sofas and slowly sip imported whiskey from crystal glasses. They are not trying to escape anything. They are just sitting in their houses, enjoying their life. But our men run off with their cheap alcohol to some dark shady place and try to drink away their troubles straight from their cheap half-bottles. They run away to drink and they drink to run away.

Still, why did Bobby drink? Why did he drink then, in June? And then now? Because I don't let him bunk school? Because I did not let him subscribe to Active Cooking? But two months ago I bought him one of the latest Micromax touch phones. And one month ago I bought him dumbbells because he said that he wants to be fit and healthy, even though I think that it is actually just to impress the girl with the green eyes at the bus stop. And last week I bought him another pair of new shoes, and even though the brand is not some big name, they are costly genuine leather shoes. So, why?

All evening I have wanted to ask that boy one question. Why did you drink? Why did you drink, my son? What did your mother do or not do that pushed you to that poison? Can you imagine this? Can you imagine a mother, a mother lying in her bed at night-time who should be thinking about what to prepare for her son's tiffin tomorrow, but who is thinking about her son drinking instead?

All evening I tiptoed around that boy. I wanted to ask him, I wanted to shout, and just now, this second, I want to wake him up and shake him hard. But I can't ask him. How can a person ask a question whose each and every answer will be wrong? So, I still just tiptoe around him quietly.

Where is my husband? Where is the father of this child? He needs to be here with his mad wife and drunken child. He needs to be here to hold his woman and thrash his son. The scene just now should be a little bit different. My husband should have come back home from the hospital in Vasant Kunj, had his tea, had his bath, then, while lying down on the divan, I would have told him about Bobby and then he would have beaten him, because it would have been his duty to beat him. And then after that, at about this time, when Bobby would have gone to sleep and the flat was dark and quiet, he would have started the washing machine and pulled me into bed without a sound and everything would have been just a little bit better.

But am I so foolish to think like this? He is just one more man, one more man who will say some useless words to me, do some stupid things to me. And then what?

16

That day when I went to Vineet's house and he cooked for me and we talked about Bobby and what not, that Thursday I did not only share my thoughts with him, but I also shared my body. Yes, I had sex with another man. And, actually, I also had sex with him yesterday, and I don't think that it was wrong.

It is not that shocking, actually. Everybody knows that everybody does it. Man or woman, everybody does it. Look at my husband. He happily told me about how the men he lives with go to some Anglo nurse from the hospital, but that he, my sweet and innocent husband, he just thinks about his wife and masturbates. Was I born yesterday? I did not ask him that day, but I want to ask him some questions now. My dear husband, when the bodies of those around you are blessed with sleep while yours lies alone on its bed restless and desperate to be held, what do you do? Tell me. Do you actually just masturbate with pictures of your faraway wife in your mind? Is that actually the truth? But what happens when your own hand is now not enough, when your body screams to be touched by a hand that is not your own? What do you do then, my dear? What do you do? You are not supposed to lie to me. And you don't need to lie. I am your wife, remember? I am your wife, and a wife knows. A wife has to understand. I see the quiet in your eyes every Friday and Sunday, I see the peace in them, the type of peace that can only come when the body is also at peace. You can tell me the truth. You are allowed to tell me that you also line up outside the Anglo nurse's room like those other men do.

I think that my husband is right about one thing. I have become a bold woman. Still, what does it actually mean? What is a bold woman? What does she do? Isn't she just a person who, like the men around her, does certain things without feeling scared? When people say, Oh, look at that woman, she is so bold, what are they saying? Actually, the only thing that they are saying is that she is not scared to make certain types of decisions. It is just like what I say about poverty, about how poverty is like being in jail and you can decide to suffer in your cell or you can decide to be free. I decided to free our family of its suffering and so I convinced my husband to go to Dubai, and many people said that I was so bold, and some people said that I had gone mad, but what do these people know? It is the same thing here. See, what did I do? I had sex with Vineet. This time it was not about my family but about my body. I decided to free my body. I decided to free my body of suffering, another type of suffering, obviously, but actually it is not that different. It is still the type of suffering that comes from the pain of need.

So, call me bold and also call me mad, because sometimes it seems that bold and mad are one and the same things, but, yes, I had sex with Vineet. And what is this thing called sex? It is just a natural thing that the body needs, like food and water. I read about it in a magazine at the clinic. A bodily need, that is what the article called it, and the article was written by an American doctor. A bodily need, that is all. If the washing machine was working, if that useless mechanic had actually come to fix it, maybe I would not have had sex with Vineet. Maybe, as I normally did, I would have just switched on the machine, and thought about my husband and me when he was still here in Delhi, and touched myself, and everything would have been fine.

Still, everything will be fine. Anybody is free to call me bold or mad or both, but nobody can point a finger at me and say that I am not still a respectable woman. And I think that Vineet is also still a respectable man. Both of us have duties to our families that we fulfil, duties to our jobs that we fulfil, and we fulfil each and every one of them without fail. So, if for just one or two hours we put those duties on one side and took off our clothes and put those down on the other side, what was wrong? Can you actually say that this, these small, little actions, made us less respectable people?

And there is one more thing that I have to tell. The day before yesterday when Bobby came back home smelling of alcohol I was very troubled. I was so troubled that I could not cook, I could not clean, I could not eat or get sleep. I had a bath, I tried my level best to pray, but nothing brought me peace. The fact that my son, Renuka Sharma's son, had drunk alcohol was already so horrible, but what made everything more difficult, much, much more difficult, was that I was all alone. The one and only other person who could have helped me, the person whose duty as the father of this boy is to discipline him and whose duty as the husband of this woman is to help her in difficult times, this person was not here.

So then what did I do? What did I do when the smell of alcohol filled my nose and made me want to vomit out each and every grain of food in my stomach? What did I do when the sight of my son made me want to catch him by his hair and throw him out on to the road? I could not call up my husband and tell him to come back and take control of his dirty son. And I did not go into the prayer room or to the temple, because we don't forget our problems, we don't forget our children, in the presence of God. I know that praying gives us great strength and without God's blessings we cannot survive, but actually, the time we spend in God's company is the time when we remember everything that troubles us. So what did I do? What could I do? I called up Vineet, because the truth is that just now no husband, no God can give me the calm that he can give me. I called up Vineet, and I told him directly that I had to see him because I needed to do what we had done that Thursday before, and he said, Fine, and he told me to meet him at his hotel on Saturday afternoon, which was yesterday.

When I got on to the train to meet Vineet, the only thing that I wanted was to have sex. All that I wanted was a man, the weight of a man, on me, and just like I wanted my body to be crushed under him, I also wanted each and every thought in my mind to be crushed. But what actually happened?

Vineet and I did have sex. Because it was the weekend and the hotel is a business hotel, many rooms were empty. Vineet kindly let me choose a room and I chose a beautiful room with a huge window from which you could see the IFFCO Chowk Metro station and the Kingdom of Dreams, which looked so grand. So, we had sex, and it was very nice, it was even nicer than the first time, but that is how it is, that is also how it was with my husband, when each time we had sex it got better and better, so we had sex, Vineet and I, but then what did I go and do after that?

I told Vineet everything. After we had sex and we were lying on that beautiful hotel bed and looking out of the window at the colourful buildings of Kingdom of Dreams, something happened to me and I said, Vineet, I have to tell you something, and he turned his eyes to me, and even though I did not see this, because how could I look at him while talking to him about such things, I could still feel his eyes on me, and then he said, Tell me.

And I told him. I told him everything. I told him that I was married and that my husband works in Dubai. I told him that Bobby is my son, not my brother, and that like him, Vineet, I don't have any brothers or sisters. I told him about my parents and my in-laws and everything. And then I said that I would understand if he was angry, even though he did not have any reason to be angry because I did not purposely lie about my life or hide anything and that actually there were many times when I had wanted to tell him everything but he had never, not even one time in all these months, bothered to ask me and so that is why I did not tell him.

And what did Vineet say to all this? What did he do? He did not shout, Whore! and catch me by my plait and throw me out on to the road. No, he did not say or do anything like that. He sat up on the bed, turned to the window, brought his feet down to the floor and stood up, each action slow and calm, not the smallest sign of anger in any of his movements, and then, like he had known everything for all these months, like he had already smelt another man on me, he gently put his hand on my shoulder and with a small smile said, Oh ho, it is all fine. And then he told me that he had to go back to work because the boss was coming soon and that I should not worry about anything and that he would call me up afterwards.

⌒

Afterwards came and afterwards went but Vineet did not call me up. Now, it is almost nine o'clock on Sunday morning, seventeen hours have passed, and he still has not called me up. Now, not only does he know my body, he knows my life. And so he won't speak to me.

Still, how does it matter? The truth is that it does not matter at all. Vineet does not matter. Who is he to me? What does he give to me that I could not find somewhere else? I could happily go to the chemist shop and buy some medicine that will make me feel good and light and calm. I could even drink some beer. Maybe I could tell Bobby to invite his mother the next time that he goes and drinks with his friends.

God, what am I saying?

God, what have I done?

17

I am fine now. By God's grace I am actually well and truly fine. I was a little bit troubled before, which I think was understandable because I am a respectable woman and respectable women normally don't do the types of things that I have been doing, but from time to time they have to do such things so that they can go on living, just like a man has to eat to live, so if I felt a little bit troubled I think that it was understandable. And if Vineet has not called me up or smsed me for four days now, it is actually better like this. Vineet Sehgal is timewaste, TV serial-type timewaste that is foolish and harmless but also dangerous because it distracts women from their duties. See, why has Bobby become the boy that he has become? Why all this cooking nonsense that he keeps talking about? Why the alcohol? What is the reason for Bobby's behaviour?

The answer is simple. The reason is me. The reason for all this is me, his mother, Renuka Sharma, who has been wasting her time with some useless man, which, if you stop for one minute and think about, is actually quite understandable, but then since when was the word understandable allowed to be used for women, especially mothers? And the truth is that no matter how understandable it was that Renuka Sharma did the types of things that she did, the truth is also that by doing such things she did not do her motherly duties properly and so her son went out of control. But by God's grace, and because of the type of person that I am, I understood this quickly, I understood that by loitering around with Vineet I put my son in danger, and now I have already started doing things to bring him back on to the straight road.

The first thing that I have started doing is spending more time with my son, so, for example, I accompanied Bobby to Ankit's father's restaurant on Monday. Bobby was not very happy when I first told him about my plan, but I begged him to let me come and he finally agreed, and I tried my level best to be jokey and fun, and I think that he was fine. Then this evening, instead of going to the market to buy rations, I stayed at home and sat with Bobby while he watched TV. Actually, it was very nice today. It was very nice to have him lying on the divan next to me with his head in my lap and to play with his hair, which, even though it is a little bit long and untidy, is so soft and beautiful. It is not black, Bobby's hair, it is actually dark brown, almost like a foreigner's or a Kashmiri's. And then yesterday I also bought Bobby the Puma-brand keds that he had been wanting for almost six months but that I had not agreed to buy because they cost almost two thousand rupees. But I decided to buy them yesterday. Actually, what happened was that last week I made a little extra money from Doctor

Sahib's ink cartridge supplier. The price of onions had gone up again, and, as I said before, this is the one and only time when I allow myself to make a little extra money, so I called up the supplier, Aggarwal, and I told him the same story that I tell all of them about how another supplier was ready to give us a huge discount, and Aggarwal begged and begged and said, Madamji, please, and I said to him, Madamji, please, what? and then after a little more talking he said, like all of them say, Madamji, we can both help each other, and then we finally agreed on an amount and completed the deal. I am sure that Doctor Sahib does not mind. When the kabaadiwallah comes to my house I don't sit on his head when he is weighing the newspapers and bottles, even though I know that he is cheating me of a few extra rupees. I say to myself, It does not matter. I will not die without twelve or fifteen rupees, but for the kabaadiwallah this money could feed his hungry child. And I think that it is one and the same thing for Doctor Sahib. What are twelve or fifteen hundred rupees to him? My father used to say, A thief is a thief, whether he steals a diamond or a cucumber, but, even though he was my father and he is dead now, I have to say that I think that he was wrong. You first need to ask the thief why he stole the cucumber. So, I made some extra money and bought Bobby the shoes that he wanted and I think that it made him a very happy boy.

I am also trying my level best to pay more attention to Bobby's studies, and this I am trying to do as carefully as I can. I am trying to do it in such a way that he does not know that I am doing it, because these days my Bobby seems to get agitated and angry easily. Sometimes I wonder what has happened to my son. Sometimes I wonder where my sweet Bobby has gone. But yes, I am trying my level best to pay more attention to Bobby's studies. I asked Rosie from the clinic what to do because her children always come first or second in class and she told me that the most important thing that I needed to do was to get *The Hindu* newspaper delivered to my house because it would greatly improve Bobby's general knowledge, which is important not only for his studies at school but for all the entrance exams that he will sit for in the future. She said that it only has proper articles in it and not all those Bollywood photos and gossip that fill up all the other newspapers, and that all South Indian families get it. Everybody knows how South Indian children are so intelligent and so good in their studies. So, *The Hindu* newspaper was delivered at seven o'clock in the morning today, it will be delivered each and every morning, and I am paying two hundred and twenty-five rupees for this, and when it came today I did not say anything to Bobby about it. I just picked up the newspaper roll from the doormat, pulled off the black rubber band, pressed the pages neat and flat with my hand, and put it carefully on top of the TV remote control on the stool next to the divan. Now I am waiting for Bobby to read it.

18

I was in the veranda picking up the dry clothes when Bobby came back home from school, and without even washing his hands and face he came outside. He greeted me and then loitered around while I was collecting the clothes. I thought that his behaviour was a little bit odd, so I said, What has happened to you today?

Nothing, Ma, he said.

Nothing. That word. I hate that word. I am scared of that word. Why not just put a black cat in my lap. I decided to keep quiet.

Ma? he said.

What? I said.

Are you angry? he said.

Not at all, I said.

Then why are you not talking? he said.

Because you said, Nothing, Ma, so I thought that you wanted me to be quiet.

Ma, please, just stop it, he said. I need to talk to you about something.

Then talk, I said, I am listening.

But you have to listen to me not only with your ears, but also with your heart, he said.

Then I knew surely that trouble was coming. But I said, Fine, and I put the bucket of clothes down on the floor and listened.

And surely trouble came. I am thinking about leaving school, Bobby said.

What? I shouted.

Ma, don't shout, please, he said, and then he took out a piece of paper from his schoolbag and gave it to me.

It was a form, an unfilled application form for a school-leaving certificate.

You have to sign it, Ma, he said.

No, that is not what I have to do. What I have to do is this, I said to Bobby, and I took the form from his hand, and then, then and there in front of that boy, I tore it up into hundreds of small, little white pieces and threw them all over the veranda railing. They fell to the road like snow.

❧

They fell to the road like snow. Such pretty words, Renuka. Your son is threatening to leave school, and this is how you talk?

In the peace of night-time, many hours after what happened on the veranda, am I trying to use pretty words to hide one very ugly truth? But poetry never hides the truth.

Seven hours have passed now since what happened in the veranda in the afternoon today, and I have still not spoken to my son. Actually, first I did not know what to say when I tore up the form and left the veranda, and then afterwards I thought that it would be better not to say anything at all because sometimes quiet is the best language to use, just like doing nothing is sometimes the best type of action. But what I did do was talk to my husband, which, obviously, was such a foolish thing to do. Actually, what happened was that I became a little bit agitated and angry, and then I thought that I should talk to my husband, I thought that he should have some idea at least about his son's behaviour because he will be in Delhi in thirty-three days' time and he should not get such a huge shock then. For all these months I have been hiding all the problems with Bobby from him because I was scared that he would just leave his job and come back. But today I thought that I would give my husband just some small, little hints so that afterwards, when he comes back, he does not fall down to the floor and hold my knees and say, Renu, what have you done? Why didn't you tell me before?

So, I called up my husband, and because it is Friday today, his off-day, I did not have to wait until night, so I called him up as soon as Bobby and I came in from the veranda and Bobby went to have his bath. And what happened? I said just one thing, just one thing about how it seems that Bobby has not been so happy at school and that he sometimes, and I especially used the word sometimes, he sometimes lies around the house with a long face. And what did my husband say? Why did I ever leave you both? he cried. What have I done? How can you manage? I will come back just now. Anyway I hate this place, I will come back now. And what not.

It took some time, but when I disconnected the phone I am quite sure that my husband was less agitated. Basically I told him that the Bobby problem was not as serious as he thought that it was but it only seemed that serious because from far away problems always seem much bigger than they actually are. And then I changed the topic to his parents in Canada and we talked about them and his sister and her house and the preparations for the baby that was going to be delivered any day now, and after all that I think I can say that my husband was calm and happy. I think I can also say that I learnt my lesson today and I swear on God, I swear on my husband himself, that I will never talk to him about such things again.

But see? Even though the main reason that I called up my husband was to prepare him a little bit for his trip to Delhi, so that he does not get too shocked by Bobby's behaviour, I also called him up for comfort because it is my right as his wife to get comfort from him. But what happened? Who had to comfort whom?

＾

Six days have passed and Vineet still has not called me up or sent me one sms. It is a little bit odd, but I have not even seen him at the Metro station. But how can this surprise me? How can I actually expect him to call me up? Still, I wish that he would call me up one time, so that I could ask him just one time why he never wants to see me again or speak to me, or touch me. I have some idea about his answer, because I have thought about it day in and day out for almost one week, and it seems that there could be two reasons. But I want to know which one of these two reasons it is. I want to know the exact answer. Is it about morals? Has the Renuka Sharma that his small eyes used to want so badly, and if anybody saw those eyes that person would know that I am not just telling stories, has that sweet Renuka Sharma turned into some dirty, shameless, used older woman that his eyes have sworn on God never to look at again? Is that the reason? Has Renuka Sharma turned into some whore? Or is it something not so deep, not so serious? Is it just that before I told him about my life I was just a pretty young woman that he met on the Metro, somebody he liked to talk to and listen to and touch and that is all and nothing else, but that now there is a new Renuka Sharma, somebody with a husband and a son and other types of problems, who he does not want to be near any more? If it is the first reason then there is nothing at all that I can do, but if it is the second reason and the problem is not me, the woman Renuka Sharma, but only the attachments to me, then I would like to tell Vineet that he does not have to worry at all. I told him about my husband and son, but this was only by mistake. This was only because of the sex, because it seems that the greatest danger of sex is that when you open your body to the man, you also open your mind to him. But that is all that it was, an opening of my mind. I want to tell Vineet that I did not actually want him to start worrying about my husband and son. I only want him to worry about this woman, this woman's body and nothing else.

And isn't this what he also wants? Can he so easily forget the two times that we were together? Can he forget the first time, the time when he invited me to his house as soon as his mother had gone out of station and how, when we were in his house, after we talked for some time he came and sat down next to me on the sofa that I was sitting on and then he suddenly put his hand on my knee and looked at me and waited to see what I would do or say and when I did not say or do anything he said, Are you scared? and I shook my head, and then he very, very slowly brought his lips to my right cheek first, then my chin and then finally my lips? Has he happily forgotten that? I remember how at that second, when he was coming to my lips so slowly, so carefully, with his eyes closed so tightly, I remember that I almost started laughing because it seemed that he was a first-timer in such things and it also seemed that he thought that I was also a first-timer, and that was actually a little bit funny. Even if he has forgotten that part, he has surely not forgotten what happened after that. I don't think that he could have forgotten what our two naked bodies did on the floor after that. And what about the second time, the last time? Vineetji, can you swear on God that you have forgotten what happened six days ago when we were locked up inside a fancy air-conditioned room in your fancy boutique hotel, when we were lying on that fancy bed with our clothes thrown all over that fancy carpet in your fancy boutique hotel?

I don't like to boast, but the truth is that after he got his first taste of me, his first touch of me, I became like his drug, I actually became like some type of addiction that made him totally mad if he could not have me. Even though we have actually only been together alone two times, there have been so many other times on the crowded train, and one time in an auto and another time behind the emergency doors at the mall, when he has tried to touch me, squeeze me, kiss me. I don't like to boast, but the truth is that if anybody at all saw how he looked at me, how he touched me, if anybody saw all this then that person would also surely think that just now, at eleven o'clock at night, Vineet is probably lying down in the darkness, his hot, hot body on his hot, hot bed, thinking of me.

19

And he was. He was thinking of me last night, and he has thought about me every night since we met each other at his hotel last Saturday. This is what he told me when we met each other at the mall today.

Yes, we met each other today. After seven days of keeping quiet, Vineet finally called me up this morning, and it was not even eight o'clock, I think, and he said that he was very, very sorry for not calling me up or smsing me for so many days, but he had been very, very busy at work and there had been a lot of tension at home. Obviously I knew that he was lying. But I was not angry. How could I be? If you give a person an elephant to swallow, if you tell him, somebody who you have given your body to, somebody who you gave your body to just one or two minutes before, if you tell him, Oh, you know, I have a husband and a child, then what can you expect? The person needs some time to digest it. So I told him that he should not worry, that I was not angry and that it was understandable that he could not talk to me for so many days. And then when he asked me if I could meet him at Select Citywalk mall in the afternoon today, I agreed.

But Vineet is an odd person sometimes. Actually, what I should say is that sometimes he behaves oddly. I had thought that when we would meet his mouth would not know what to say, his eyes would not know where to look, his hands would not know what to do with this new woman standing in front of him, this new used woman. But when he met me at the Metro station, it seemed as if I was the sweet same Renuka from the week before, the girl of his dreams, that sweet Renuka who was probably just twenty-five years of age and worked in a doctor's office, that sweet Renuka who probably lived with her parents and brother somewhere near the Hauz Khas Metro station. When he met me it seemed as if there was no husband and child. It seemed as if it was still only Vineet and me in this world.

I have spent many hours at night-time, when sleep will not come, thinking about why I like to meet Vineet, why I waste such a lot of time loitering around with him, and I think I finally understand the reason now. When we are together it is only the two of us in this world. No husband, no child, no in-laws. I know that I am not supposed to say this, but the truth is that when I am with Vineet I totally forget them all, all my family, except for the two or three times that I have talked about Bobby. Maybe this is what it feels like to be on holiday, the type of holiday that my husband keeps telling me to take when he thinks that I am feeling too tense or worried about something. But Sharma Sahib, I am not like your stupid lizards any more. I know how to slip away.

So we met each other outside the Metro station, Vineet and I, and from there we decided to take an auto to the mall, and even there at the mall for the three hours that we spent walking around all the beautiful showrooms, or sitting, sitting and talking, sitting and eating, or sometimes just sitting quietly, even there it seemed as if it was only him and me, it seemed as if the words that I had spoken the Saturday before had never been spoken and my husband and son still remained hidden deep inside me. It was so nice, I was feeling so calm and happy, but then when we left the mall and started walking towards the Metro station, Vineet suddenly, just like that, said, How is Bobby? I pretended that I had not heard him, but again he said, How is Bobby? Actually, it did not happen exactly like that. Actually, as we first started walking, Vineet said, I want to take you on a holiday to the mountains. The mountains? I said. Yes, he said, I remember how you told me that you wanted to see snow, so I talked to Neha's brother, who is a travel agent, and he told me that Rohtang Pass, which is near Manali, has snow even in summer, and there are very nice, modern Volvo buses to Manali with clean toilets and DVD players, and it is only a twelve-hour overnight journey from here. Before I could answer, Vineet then said, And don't worry, we can take Bobby with us, and then again, before I could say something, Vineet said, How is Bobby?

How is Bobby? I wanted to shout. I wanted to shout, Stop! I wanted to tell Vineet that this was already a holiday for me, this, these moments alone with him, away from all my problems, away from my Bobby, this was enough of a holiday, and I did not need to go all the way to Manali, as long as Vineet did not ask about Bobby. But again Vineet said, How is Bobby?

Vineet did not understand that it was after so many days that my mind felt free when I was with him today, and that I did not want this short time of calm and happiness to end. He did not understand that I just wanted this little holiday from my useless son to go on for a little bit more time, and so I just said to Vineet, He is fine, Bobby is well and truly fine, and since we were walking by Max Super Speciality Hospital at that time, I quickly tried to talk about it instead, and I told him how my friend Rosie brought me here last year to show it to me and it was so beautiful inside, and so clean, that for one or two seconds I had thought that I was standing in the middle of the Taj Palace Hotel. And the hospital actually was just like a five-star hotel and just like a five-star hotel it had a fancy reception and lobby, and staff who were dressed in very smart and stylish uniforms, and I was telling Vineet all this, and I also told him about how Doctor Sahib is a Senior Consultant here, and I kept blabbering on and on because I was hoping that Vineet would forget about the Bobby topic, but what can I say? He kept coming back to the topic. He did not understand. Just like each and every man that I know, Vineet did not understand that from time to time there are things other than her children that a woman thinks about, that from time to time there are things other than her children that make a woman happy.

Finally I gave up. I gave up, and I don't know why but I told Vineet about how Bobby had suddenly told me yesterday that he wanted to leave school. And Vineet said some useful things.

He said that I should be careful about how I react. Children these days don't obey the stick, he said. They obey reason. And he gave me some more examples from his own life. I know that a man without a child is actually just a child himself, no matter how old he is, but I understood the value of his words. The only problem is that these were not the type of words that I wanted from him. Actually, the truth is that I did not want any words at all from him, but if words were the only things that we had this afternoon, then at least they should have been about the actions that they were substituting for.

⌒

We took some photos. Vineet took photos of me sitting by the fountains outside the mall, standing on the escalator inside it, and a few other photos. He also made me take photos of him on my phone, one in front of the Nike showroom and two of him leaning against a fancy red SUV. There is also one photo on my phone that he took of both of us eating ice cream at the food court, both of us smiling. It is in front of me now, this photo of Vineet and me. I am going to delete it, and all the others, and not because of Bobby. Bobby could not care about his mother just now, he would not even care if his mother was with another man. Bobby is too busy in his own world, too busy thinking about cooking and leaving school. Just like Bobby is too busy to study or read the newspaper that I especially subscribed to for him, Bobby is too busy to think about his mother. No, I will delete the photos because I hate photos, all photos. Look at this photo of Vineet and me, leaning into each other, eating strawberry ice cream, smiling, smiling like a young, happily married couple. I am young in this photo. I am wearing the yellow and orange suit that I bought in Lajpat Nagar last summer. I look as young as Vineet. Look at this photo. What story does it tell? It seems that after the photo is taken, this nice young couple will walk back to their flat somewhere nearby and quietly unlock the door because there is nobody inside, and then they will take off all their clothes without words or worry and do the thing that they want to do more than anything else in the whole world, the thing that Vineet and I had actually wanted to do but could not do today. See? Photos are lies. Stories. And what about these other photos here in front of me that my husband put in frames and hung on the wall above our bed even though I begged him and begged him not to do that. Here on the left, my sweet Bobby at age four in his coat and tie, and next to this, a studio photo of my husband and me with baby Bobby in my arms, and there, up there on the right below the tube light, in black and white, my mother and father, alive. Photos will tell you lies, photos will break your heart.

20

I have never been on a holiday, actually, except for my honeymoon, seventeen years ago, when my husband and I went to Jaipur, and we went alone, without any family members, and we stayed in a hotel so there was no cooking or cleaning, and in the daytime we came to know the city and at night-time we came to know each other. It is a nice thing to do, a holiday. Doctor Sahib takes many holidays, and almost every one of them abroad. It is actually like running away. I am sure that you have seen those advertisements that travel agents put in magazines and newspapers, advertisements like European Getaway or Tropical Escape or Mountain Hideaway, and what not. Why are these holidays given such names? These companies understand that people want to get away from their problems, they want to escape and hide from all their big and small problems. So, in our early married life whenever my husband suggested that we go on a holiday I just said no because at that time it did not seem that there was any big problem to run away from and also it seemed foolish to spend such a lot of money just to see some new place when you could see so many new and different places on TV. But now it is different. Now, by God's grace, my husband has a good job in Dubai and so I have a little bit of money. Now, I also have problems that I want to run away from. But does this mean I will just get up and go on a holiday with some man that I met on the Metro?

No.

See, whatever you do, good or bad, right or wrong, it is very, very important to set limits. And I know my limits, and I have set them. I can meet Vineet from time to time, enjoy his mind, enjoy his body. But I am a good woman. I have a child and a husband and in-laws and a job, and I have duties towards each and every one of these, and I don't like to boast, but the truth is that I have always fulfilled my duties without fail and I will keep fulfilling my duties until the day that I die. Nobody, and surely not Vineet, can ever stop me, and so, obviously not, I will not just forget everything and go on a stupid holiday just like that with Vineet.

The truth is that I am quite shocked that Vineet could think such thoughts, and I am even more shocked that he could share such thoughts with me. It is one thing that he suggested that we, Vineet and I, go on a holiday, but he also dared to suggest that we take my son with us! Has he gone mad? Does he think that I have gone mad? See, to some extent I can understand that a young man can have foolish romantic thoughts, even though Vineet is actually not that young. I can try to understand that he has dreams about being with me in the mountains, sitting by the fire, lying naked with me in a warm bed, rolling around in the snow, and what not. But how, how could he want to pull Bobby into this dream? This thing that Vineet and I share, this relationship, or whatever it is that you want to call it, this is about a modern man and a modern woman and sex and a certain type of friendship, and that is all. Nothing else, nobody else, and surely not my son. Doesn't Vineet understand this? Isn't this what he also wants?

Maybe Vineet is confused. Maybe he thinks that the only way to make me part my legs is through my child, that if he talks about my dear son Bobby he can make me do whatever he wants. But, whatever the reason is for Vineet always wanting to talk about Bobby, and now, wanting to invite him on a holiday, which, even after twenty-four hours, I still just cannot believe, whatever it is, Vineet better understand, and understand once and for all, that I will not allow it. I will not allow him to pull my son into this thing. I know that one or two times I was the one to bring up the topic of Bobby, and it was foolish of me, I know, and I know that Vineet gave me some good advice. But not any more. I swear on God that I will never ever bring up the topic of Bobby again, and I will also not allow him to try to talk to me about Bobby ever again. It is one thing if a third person tries to push himself between husband and wife, but it is a totally different thing if he tries to come between parent and child. Bobby is the son of Dheeraj Sharma and that is a God-given fact. Vineet cannot change that, and I will show him gently that he actually does not need to do that. My legs

will part even without any talk of Bobby. Actually, my legs
will part only without any talk of Bobby.

Seducing a woman through her child? I know that most people
would probably be very shocked by all this. But I would like
to explain something here, about marriages in these modern
times, and even though I am going to sound like a child who
uses the idea of modern times as an excuse for behaving badly,
I am sure that it will be clear that this is not what I am trying to
do. What I want to say here is that these are modern times and
in these modern times modern husbands and modern wives are
sometimes forced to live separately, but even if their marriages
are different to the marriages of their parents and grandparents,
their needs, their needs for love and friendship and sex, are not
any different. They are still just men and women with hearts
and minds and bodies that have grown up needs. For example,
that Anglo nurse that my husband said his roommates go to,
and that I am sure my husband also goes to. Far away from
their wives this is what they do. What else can they do? Can
we blame them? Should we stop them? Wouldn't it be like
telling them not to eat? There is this Internet site called Human
Digest. It is full of stories of sex, all types of sex, and I know
about this only because my husband showed it to me one time
many years ago. So there are all these stories of sex, and many
of these stories, more than half of them, I am sure, are either
about husbands who are working in the Gulf without family
doing what not with strangers, or about wives left behind in

India doing what not with their brothers-in-law or servants or neighbours. Now I am not a vulgar woman like some of the vulgar people in these stories who do the types of things that I cannot even speak about, and my husband is also not a vulgar man, so actually I should not compare myself or my husband to the people on this site, but I just want to show that from time to time men and women do these types of things, and they only do them because they have to, not because they want to. The first law of marriage is being together, and if that law has to be broken, as it had to be broken with my husband and me and so many other married couples because we all understood that it was necessary for a better life, if that law of togetherness has to be broken, then other laws of marriage are also automatically broken. That is how it is, in these modern times. And nobody actually wants to do this. Nobody actually wants to slip into a stranger's bed, nobody actually wants to hide. That is the truth, nobody wants to tell lies.

21

I have brought up my son well, I know. But good manners can only control how you show your anger, they don't make the anger itself go away. Even though you will not raise your voice at grown ups, because your mother has taught you not to do that, it does not mean that you will not find some other way to show the anger that boils inside you. Today, my well-mannered son showed me his anger. Obviously he did say sorry afterwards, but politely and gently my son showed me his anger today. He had come back very late from the restaurant, even though he knows that he has to be back in the house by seven o'clock latest so that he has enough time for his studies. This was one of my conditions for allowing him to go. But still, he came back home at almost eight thirty today. So I was very angry, obviously, and obviously I scolded him just like any dutiful mother would scold her child. And then what happened? After I scolded him, Bobby looked straight into my eyes and very softly said, Ma, I wish you were the one who had gone to Dubai. That is exactly what he said.

Even though I know that he is just a child, I felt such a lot of pain. He could have just stolen a knife from that stupid restaurant he goes to and stabbed his mother in the heart instead. Children don't understand how much they can hurt their mothers. Or maybe they do understand and that is why they do it.

But the truth is that from time to time I also wish the same. I also wish sometimes that I was the one who had gone to Dubai. It would have been so nice. Even if my husband says that it hardly feels like a foreign place and that it is only like a clean India, at least it is clean. And I would have taken evening walks on Jumeirah Beach and earned a lot of money of my own and only worried about my son from far, far away. It would have been so nice. I would have felt so free. And maybe being far, far away, my son would have understood the value of his mother.

It is an odd thing, this mother and child relationship. And so difficult. We are taught, we are taught by our fathers and mothers and textbooks and teachers, that every relationship is based on giving and taking. You give something to somebody and then you receive something from that person. You get something from somebody and then you quickly give back something. And if one side stops, then the relationship stops. Simple. That is how it is, that is how the world works. Every relationship in my life, and not just between my husband and me, or my parents and me, but even between Doctor Sahib and me, Rosie and me, even Vineet and me, has been like this, giving and taking. The five or six people in my life who did not give me something back in return for what I gave them, like one nurse Mariam who used to work at the clinic, or my father's brother and his family, I just stopped talking to these people. My mother was an only child like me and the only relatives I had were my father's brother and his family, but even then, because my uncle and his horrible wife and children only took, took, took from me and never gave me anything, any love, even then, when I had nobody, I still just stopped talking to them, and today, in my mind, they are dead. All dead. Because Renuka Sharma is not a fool. She will not allow anybody to treat her badly. And, mark my words, if tomorrow my husband tried to do the same thing as those relatives, even he, my husband, would find himself in the same hole as them.

But what can I say? All these grand, grand words I speak like I am some grand, grand woman, these words mean nothing when I am face to face with my son. These words become dust.

I remember when Bobby was a baby. I would feed Bobby and bathe him and play with him and stay awake night after night looking after him, and, yes, my husband did try his level best to help, but how much can a man actually do? And what happened? The first word that came out of Bobby's baby mouth was Papa. Mummy did all the work, but Papa was the word. And then it was Papa, Papa, Papa, day in and day out. I did everything for that boy, I broke my back for him, but still, Papa. Always Papa. The boy gave his mother nothing. For a long time not even that one word Mummy. And it is not any different these days. What do I get from him now? Still nothing. And what do I want? All that I want is that he should eat properly, sleep properly and study properly. That is all. But all that I get are painful words, words like knives.

There are one or two things that I would like to ask my son. There are one or two things that I want to know. Bobby, my dear son, you are, you know, a healthy, handsome, intelligent boy, and everybody says this. Now, tell me, do you think that this just happened by magic? Do you think that you are what you are today, the envy of every mother, just like that? Or do you understand that there is this person in your life, your mother, who has spent every second of her life from the day you were born trying to make you into this healthy, handsome, intelligent boy? Do you even know that your mother exists? Bobby, my dear and loving son, I also wish that I went to Dubai instead of your father because it seems that a child will only see his mother when she is not there.

So, the law of give and take is broken in a mother and child relationship. And then the most difficult part is that a mother cannot just say, Oh, I am being treated so badly that this relationship is finished now! How can she do that? She is a mother! A goddess! She will give, give and give. She will suffer quietly and live.

Maybe God created a special type of heart just for women, a mother heart that only needs to give to beat, a heart that needs nothing else, and that is why mothers don't run away. And maybe God also created a special type of mother mind that will always and only think about her child with love and forgiveness, and that is why now, at this very second, as I think again about what happened today, about what Bobby said to me, now, I am starting to forget those words, I am starting to forget the pain, and the only thing that my mind is now remembering are the moments after he said those horrible things, the time when I refused to eat my food and I just sat on the divan and picked up *The Hindu* newspaper and tried to read it, and then my sweet Bobby came and sat down on the floor at my feet and started pressing my legs, and then he just looked up at me and said, Ma, if you don't eat, then I won't eat.

That is all that this mother mind remembers now, so that the giving can go on.

⌐

I have decided to change my life a little bit. I have decided that I am going to forget about all this disciplining business with Bobby and let his father do all that when he comes back. I am going to have fun, because sometimes it seems that I will forget what it feels like to have fun, and I am only thirty-seven years of age and I don't want to be like old people because for them everything good and fun and happy are just pictures in their minds, pictures from the past. No, I am going to have fun with my Bobby, and I will also go on having fun with Vineet until my husband comes back, because fun with Vineet is actually like a tonic for me, it is like taking Chyawanprash to keep fit and healthy, and then, when my husband comes back, which is in just twenty-eight days' time, I will also have a lot of fun with him.

22

Vineet has finally bought his flat. It is in a complex called Sunshine Boulevard in Greater Noida. It is the one that I liked best. He took me there to see it yesterday. He has bought unit number twenty-two, because two plus two adds up to four, and in numerology four is for people who are steady and patient and practical, people who want to achieve their goals. That is what a vaastu expert told him. The flat doesn't actually look much like the show flat that we had seen before, and the complex itself is not as fancy as the photos in the brochure, but they say that all builders and developers are big cheats and this is how it is. Still, I like the flat, and I think that his mother will also like it. There are two bedrooms with built-in cupboards, and one of them, the master bedroom, has an attached bathroom with tiles that have little purple and yellow butterflies that look so pretty. The kitchen is quite big. It is a modular kitchen, and it has all these nice cabinets and drawers that are painted red. There is also an exhaust fan above the window, which is important. The hall is a little bit small, but they have installed a very beautiful ceiling fan there, the type that has crystal lights hanging from it. It almost looks like a chandelier.

There are six towers in the complex and each of them has fifteen floors. In the small area in the middle, surrounded by the towers, there is a nice children's park with swings, seesaws, a slide and a big jungle gym. It is good that the park is located here because mothers can watch their children play directly from their kitchen windows. On the ground floor of Tower One there is a recreation room with a table tennis table and some sofas for residents to sit and talk to their neighbours. There is also quite a lot of parking space, but only for residents. Visitors have to park their vehicles outside the gate. The complex is quite nice, actually.

So he took me to see his new flat, but just like the last two or three times that we have been together, something odd happened. To some extent I could even say that something funny happened. We were in the master bedroom and I was standing near the door to the bathroom, when suddenly he said, Tell me one thing, Renu. You love your child, no?

I kept quiet.

From the way that you talk about Bobby, it seems that you love children, he said.

I nodded my head in some vague type of way and still kept quiet.

Children are beautiful, he said. They are proof of their parents' love, and they make their parents' love stronger.

I almost wanted to laugh at all this Bollywood dialogue but I stopped myself.

And then he walked up to where I was standing and put one hand on my shoulder, and said, Renu, this is the room where we will start our family.

Now I could not stop myself and I burst out laughing.

This is not a joke, he said. You and I are going to get married. I think that you know me now and you know that I will never say or do anything without thinking about it carefully from all sides. Now, I am telling you, you and I should get married as soon as you get a divorce from your husband.

I tried to stop my laughing because I understood that he was actually being serious, and then I tried to find some words to answer him, but before I could find them he starting talking again.

And don't worry about Bobby, he said. I will look after him. And don't worry about my mother. She is actually quite broadminded. My cousin married a boy from the North East and my mother was the only person in the whole family who accepted the boy. It will probably take her some time, but I know my mother, and I know that in the end she will love you and respect you.

I did not want to spoil this time that we had together. We were together alone after such a long time and I still had to take off all my clothes and lie down on the nice new tiled floor and pull him down to me. So, even though I only felt like laughing at all his nonsense, and telling him that maybe he should try to be more broadminded and modern like he thinks his mother is, I did not do or say all that because I knew that he would feel very bad and then we would just leave and go home. Instead of all that, I told him, trying to make my voice sound as serious as his voice, that just like he had thought about it so carefully, I also needed to do the same, I also needed time to think, and then I did what I had planned to do and took off my clothes and his clothes, and then we had a very nice time together.

꙳

When I came back home I decided that Bobby and I should have some fun and so I suggested to him that since his father was going to come back in just twenty-five days' time, we should at least visit the new airport one time so that we know exactly where to go and what to do on 31 August 2011. And my Bobby agreed.

What an airport it is! I remember when my husband and Bobby and I first saw the mall buildings in Saket. For a few seconds we could not speak. We almost could not breathe because we had only seen such beautiful buildings in foreign places on TV. It was hard to believe that such buildings could actually be standing just twenty minutes away from us by scooter. That is how Bobby and I felt today. This new airport is much more beautiful and modern than the old airport we saw when my husband left for Dubai in 2009. It is called Terminal 3 and I am sure that it is as good as any airport abroad. It seems to be built with only glass and steel. I don't remember seeing any cement at all! And it feels like you are in a foreign country. Actually, no, not a foreign country but some place more distant, some place in space. And then there is this other building, separate from the main airport building, which is only for parking. A building with six or seven floors, only for parking!

There was a lot of security all around. Even one kilometre before you reached the building there were police check posts checking each and every vehicle that was going to the airport. And around the airport building itself, any side that you looked there were policemen, policewomen, commandos and what not. And I used to think that the malls have too much security! But it is fully understandable. Terminal 3 is well and truly something that our nation should be proud of, like the Taj Mahal or Rashtrapathi Bhavan or Select Citywalk. And it deserves the same type of protection from terrorists as those buildings, because what Doctor Sahib says is very true. Even though it happened far away from us, India has changed since those Muslim men crashed planes into those buildings in America.

⌒

It is eleven o'clock and the power has gone. It has been gone for almost two hours now. We have an inverter, my husband bought it for us before he left, but the battery has drained and so I can't switch on the fan. And even though it is August, there has been no rain for almost ten days. It is so hot. Every part of my body that is touching the bed is wet with sweat. It is so hot that I cannot get sleep.

But my Bobby sleeps peacefully here on his folding cot. He sleeps peacefully because his mother has been keeping quiet, his mother has been good to him. But am I actually being good by keeping quiet and not guiding him back towards the straight road? Isn't it a crime to not stop a crime? Don't you become as much of a criminal as the criminal himself? I don't know, but whatever it is or whoever I have to become, and I would become a murderer if that was the only way, all that I want is to see my Bobby happy in the day and peaceful at night-time.

23

I know that from time to time I have said that Sundays are boring, but I never understood until today that a boring Sunday can actually be a great blessing. Today started just like all Sundays. In the morning I did all my chores, and Bobby, even though he did not open his textbooks, he actually picked up the newspaper and seemed to be reading it quite carefully. We also Skyped with my husband as we do every Friday and Sunday, and today he looked much better. My husband looked less sad, less tired. He said that he has a new boss, an Arab also, obviously, but an Arab who hates Indians less. This Arab is very rich, my husband said. He eats fifteen or twenty almonds at one time, just like that. He eats almonds like peanuts. My husband said that he has seen it with his own two eyes. And then my husband said that just like me, he is also counting the days for 31 August 2011. He said that as soon as his plane lands, the first thing he wants to do is come home and eat a meal cooked by his wife, and then he wants to go with Bobby and me to India Gate for ice cream. He said that he has this picture in his mind of the three of us in an auto, and it is raining, and he is sitting in the middle with his wife on one side of him and his son on the other side of him. He said that these days this picture comes to his mind every time he closes his eyes.

I almost started crying when he said this, but I controlled myself. I quickly started to talk about one news item instead, this horrible news item that the nurses were talking about in the clinic last month, about this young boy who sold his kidney to buy an iPhone because his parents did not have the money to buy it for him. I think that this was a good thing that I did. It was important for me to talk about this to remind both my husband on the monitor and my son sitting next to me why we have to live like this just now.

So, everything was normal, everything had that Sunday feeling, and after all my morning chores I had to go for Rosie's daughter's wedding. I asked Bobby to come with me but he said that he was tired, and I did not want to force him, so I went alone. The wedding was in a church near Connaught Place, and it was the first time that I had attended a Christian wedding ceremony, and even though it was quiet and everybody looked serious, even then, it was actually quite nice. And Doctor Sahib sat down next to me during the ceremony. There were many, many empty seats, but Doctor Sahib came and sat down next to me. So everything felt good and nice, and I was feeling very calm and happy, and I came back home and knocked on the door, because I always make Bobby latch it from inside, and Bobby opened the door, but then what do I see? In the hall, in my house, sitting on the divan side by side, who do I see?

It was Vineet, Vineet and that stupid friend of his Neha. In my house.

I thought that I was going to have a heart attack. My heart hit so hard and fast against my chest that I thought that then and there I would fall down to the floor. But I just walked into the flat quietly and smiled at everybody, and very calmly, very coolly and calmly, I turned to Bobby and said, Have you offered them some tea?

Bobby nodded his head, and Vineet said, He made us such tasty tea, and then Neha said, What a nice boy you have.

I sat down on the stool and smiled again. What else could I do?

After a few seconds, Vineet stood up and, fixing his eyes on my eyes, he said, We have to go now, but we will meet you at the clinic tomorrow.

And they left. Then after about five minutes I received an sms from Vineet. He said that he told Bobby that he and Neha work with me at Doctor Sahib's clinic and that he just wanted to drop off some sweets to celebrate the purchase of his new flat. I deleted the sms and then after that I did not know what to do, but then Bobby switched on the TV and I sat down next to him and did some deep breathing.

So what did you read in the newspaper this morning? I said, after some time.

Different things, Bobby said.

Like what? I said.

Politics, he said.

Reading the newspaper is a good daily habit, I said.

Then Bobby said, Those people are very nice.

They are quite nice, I said.

Is Neha Didi Vineet Bhaiya's girlfriend? he said.

Maybe, I said.

Why didn't Rosie Aunty invite them for the wedding? he said.

I thought that I would have another heart attack, but then I thought of an answer. Rosie Aunty's husband only allowed her to invite Doctor Sahib and me, I said.

Then Bobby said, Did you know that Vineet Bhaiya has some professional training as a chef?

I wanted to shout, Vineet Bhaiya? He is not your Vineet Bhaiya! But I said, He has talked about food from time to time.

He told me that he can cook all types of Indian and Chinese and Continental dishes, Bobby said.

I think that it is just timepass for him, I said.

That is because his father did not allow him to become a chef, Bobby said. But he has offered to give me cooking classes. Then Bobby smiled and got up, and went to the fridge and took out a box of sweets. Vineet Bhaiya brought this for you, he said. He has bought a new flat.

⌐

I should join Bollywood. The way I acted today, the way I acted so cool and calm, I should get the Filmfare award for Best Actress. A man that I met on the Metro, a man who is not my son's father but who I have sex with even then, this man was happily sitting in my house talking away to my son, and I acted as if this was such a normal thing, I acted as if our neighbour had just dropped in to show me the water bill. What a grand performance, Renuka Sharma! You should be so proud of yourself!

⌒

The whole afternoon I watched Bobby carefully. I knew that he would not say anything to me directly, but, obviously, I wanted to know if he suspected anything of Vineet and Neha's visit, so I watched carefully for any odd signs coming from him. By God's grace, he acted very normally and when I was fully convinced that everything was fine, I told him that I would make him kheer, his favourite sweet dish, and I sent him off to the market to buy some milk. I had thought that while Bobby was out of the house I would call up Vineet.

I had thought that I would call up Vineet and shout at him. How dare you meet my son without asking me? I thought I would say. Why are you pulling my son into this? And how dare you come to my house and, on top of that, bring that woman with you?

But before I called him up I did some deep breathing and I thought about everything, and then I very quickly understood that it is not Vineet that I should be angry with, it is myself. My father used to say, The eyes will not see what the mind does not want them to. But today my mind has ordered my eyes to see the truth. And the truth is that the only reason that Vineet was sitting in my house today and talking to my son is because I invited him. See, wasn't it me who first went running to him when I had problems with Bobby? Wasn't it me who first asked Vineet for advice about Bobby? Isn't that an invitation into my home?

It is also a sign, I think, this behaviour, a sign to Vineet that all that matters to this woman is her son, and so if he wants to be with her he has to show interest in her son. See? I cannot blame him. The only person I can point a finger at is myself.

Still, what has happened has happened. We have to look forward, and I will make sure that Vineet understands that he does not need to involve himself with Bobby just to be with me.

24

More than one time I have said that I have to keep Vineet away from Bobby because Bobby is my husband's son and because this relationship is only about Vineet and me and nobody else and especially not my child. I know that I have said all this. But I think that I have changed my mind. And I know that what I am going to say will sound a little bit odd, but what made me change my mind was actually my Bobby. Since Vineet came to our flat four days' ago, Bobby has been pestering me day in and day out to call up Vineet for those cooking classes and, until this evening, each time Bobby has asked me to call him up, I have refused. But then when I was sitting quietly in the prayer room this afternoon, my mind became clearer in the presence of God, and I decided that there is actually nothing wrong in allowing them to meet each other. Just by giving Bobby cooking classes, Vineet is not going to become Bobby's father. And teaching a child to cook is hardly a fatherly thing to do anyway. And if Bobby spends a little bit of time with

Vineet and me, that is hardly pulling him into our relationship, or whatever it is that you want to call it. The only thing is that Bobby must never ever know about this relationship. That is the main thing. That is what I have to be very, very careful about.

Apart from that, what is there to worry about? Bobby will see that his mother has a friend who is a man. Is that going to shock him? And what will he do? Call up his father? And will his father also get shocked? It is the twenty-first century. Even a good woman can be friends with a man.

So after I came out of the prayer room with my new decision, I told Bobby about it, and, what can I say? Bobby was so happy, so happy. He gave me such a big hug that I almost fell down. This in itself made me very happy, but then Bobby promised me something that made me even happier. He said that if the cooking classes go nicely, then he would stop going to that restaurant in Saket. All that I could do was look up and thank God.

Then I had to call up Vineet, because Bobby would not let me do anything else until I talked to his Vineet Bhaiya. With Bobby sitting on my head I felt quite nervous, but I picked up my phone, and in less than two rings, I could hear Vineet's hello. It was much more nervous than my hello. I think that he thought that I was still angry with him for coming to our flat. We have not had the chance to talk properly since that day. But I tried to keep my voice friendly and steady, and without wasting any time I told him that Bobby, my son, was here with me and how he wanted very much for Vineet to give him cooking classes whenever it was convenient. When I said this it seemed as if I had told him he had won the lottery. I could almost see him jump. Yes, yes! he said. When should I come? Tomorrow? The day after? When? When? When?

If I had allowed Vineet or Bobby to decide the date, there would be a storm in my kitchen just now. But Saturday evening has been fixed. Vineet is actually on duty at his hotel that day, but he said that he has so many days of casual leave remaining that his boss cannot stop him.

25

If I ever complain that I don't have any fun, I should be given one tight slap and reminded about last evening when Vineet came for the cooking class. What fun it was! Even for me. Even though I had to stand quietly and watch my son, my own son, sweating in the kitchen as he chopped vegetables and grated paneer and kneaded dough, even though I had to watch him stand for hours and hours in front of the hot stove and then on his knees cleaning the kitchen floor, even then all that I can say is that we all had such a lot of fun last evening.

Vineet brought all the ingredients with him, and I am sure that he must have spent almost one thousand rupees. So, first he sat down with Bobby and he had a long, long talk with him. He told him that he would start him with some basic Indian cooking techniques, which Bobby did not seem very happy about, because Bobby thinks that he knows quite a lot about Indian dishes already, but Bobby is a good boy, a good student, and he kept quiet and listened carefully. Then Vineet talked about some general topics, about how important it is to respect the great chefs and their methods, for example, and about how only after you are sure, one hundred per cent sure, that you have mastered a recipe, only then should you try to be creative. He also told Bobby about how important it is to be organised and methodical, and to keep your kitchen neat and clean. The kitchen is your temple, Vineet said.

I was not allowed into the kitchen at all. They insisted that I relax in the hall in front of the TV. Obviously I could not do that, how could I? So, I just stood at the kitchen door and watched quietly.

What happened in my kitchen was better than any cooking show that I have ever seen. They worked quietly and methodically. I was totally wrong to think that there would be a storm in my kitchen. There was no banging and shouting, and even though they were cooking so many different things all at the same time in such a small, little kitchen, there was never ever any mess. And Vineet's teaching method was so good. He would give Bobby some long instructions on something, he would explain everything so patiently, and Bobby would stand quietly and listen. Then Vineet would show Bobby something, and Bobby would watch him carefully and repeat it. The truth is that even I, a woman, learnt quite a few things about cooking from Vineet. I almost went to get an exercise book to take notes! I know that this sounds funny, but how many women know that when you want to grind cashew nuts in a mixie, all that you have to do is add a pinch of flour so that they don't stick to the mixie container? How many women know that when you cut garlic, the best way to get the smell off your hands is by rubbing them on any stainless steel item?

The dishes that these two cooked in my kitchen were tastier than anything I have ever eaten. Even though they were everyday items, like dal and vegetables and paneer, pulao and salad, there was nothing everyday in their taste. I am sure that even a man like Doctor Sahib, who has eaten in every fancy restaurant in Delhi, who has probably eaten in every fancy restaurant in every city in the world, and I know this because I manage all his credit card payments, even Doctor Sahib, I am sure, would say that these dishes that Vineet and Bobby prepared were well and truly special.

After we all ate, and they had made me eat first, the two of them washed all the pots and pans and plates and cleaned up the whole kitchen, and I should say that the kitchen looked so good that it seemed as if I was the one who had done the cleaning. Then the three of us sat down in the hall.

For some time nobody talked. We just sat quietly, looking up and looking down. This made me worried. I wanted it to feel like a normal thing, like when some neighbour or relative comes to visit. But the thing is that nobody actually ever visits us. I don't have any relatives, and none of my husband's relatives live in Delhi, and when a neighbour comes to the flat, they just stand at the door to give me a bill, or return the torch or whatever that they borrowed. This is an odd thing. And I never realised this before. Still, I wanted it to feel like a normal thing, I wanted Bobby to feel like this was a normal thing, so I quickly thought and thought about what to talk about, and, by God's grace, I thought of the computer that Doctor Sahib is supposed to buy for me, so then I told them, both Vineet and Bobby, that since they both know much more about computers than I know, they could help me decide which model I should tell Doctor Sahib to get for me.

This was a very good idea because then, for the next one and a half hours, this is what we talked about, the computer. We had to go into the bedroom, that is where our computer is. Bobby and I sat on the bed, and Vineet sat on the chair in front of the computer, and together we looked at many different, different desktop models on the Internet. Vineet thought that I should give Doctor Sahib some options in case there are availability problems with the vendor, so we made a shortlist of four models, one HP, two Dells and one Lenovo. There was this beautiful one from Apple that all three of us liked so much, but it was so costly that I did not put it on the list. Doctor Sahib would think that I have gone mad.

There was quite a lot of laughing and joking when Vineet was here, and this, obviously, was nice in some way, and I understood that my Bobby needs company from time to time, but now I am a little bit worried by this. I know that just by laughing and joking with Bobby, Vineet cannot become his father, but I don't want them to get too close. But I should not worry too much. Most of the time Vineet was very professional with Bobby. Still, maybe I should encourage Bobby to become friendly with the girl with the green eyes at the bus stop. I know that I sound like I have gone mad, but if you stop for one minute and think about it, think about it as a modern person in modern times, what is actually wrong with boys and girls being friends? This girl, more than Vineet, is probably the type of company that Bobby needs. As long as she does not interfere with my Bobby's studies and career, which, from how neat and clean she looks, from how neat and clean her father looks, she surely would not do, I think that it would be good for him to have a nice girl in his life as a friend. Actually, I think that it is good for everybody to have a friend.

So, after Vineet left, which was around ten o'clock, Bobby and I had our baths and changed our clothes, and came into the bedroom. Then, while I was hemming one of my kurtas and Bobby was writing something in his exercise book, Bobby suddenly looked up at me and said, Ma, can you promise me one thing?

You know that I can't promise anything until you first tell me what it is, I said.

Can you promise me that you will not tell Papa about Vineet Bhaiya and the cooking classes? Maybe he won't like it.

This was almost funny. Wasn't I supposed to be the one asking for such a promise? But I just said, Fine, I will see, and then I put away my sewing kit and pretended to go to sleep.

26

It seems that I will never see Vineet again. It is sad, but it seems that whatever it is that Vineet and I had, these nice five months that we spent together, it is all finished. The day before yesterday, when I had come back from the clinic and Bobby had come back from school, and we were sitting together and eating our lunch, Bobby told me, just like that, in a calm, cool voice, about how he had met Vineet two times since their cooking class last Sunday. He said that for both meetings he had got a gate pass from school, children from the eleventh and twelfth standards are allowed to do that, he said, and that both times he only bunked his PT class because he knew that I would have got very angry if he had bunked any proper class. And then he told me about how both times they sat at a tea stall in Sheikh Sarai and talked and talked about cooking and life and what not.

Now, I was angry with Bobby, obviously. I was happy that he had not bunked his Maths or Physics class, but still, any type of bunking is wrong. But what actually made my blood boil was Vineet. Not only did he make my son bunk school, which was already a horrible thing to do, but Vineet also met my son without telling me. Vineet met my son behind my back. Vineet lied to me.

Vineet and I had not met in the five days since he came to the flat because he was on evening shift at the hotel, but we did talk on the phone two or three times and he still never said anything, not one word, about meeting Bobby. But I should say one thing here. On Wednesday, when Bobby had come back from school, I thought that I could smell Vineet's cologne, but then I just let it be, because it seemed that it was just one of those foolish things that happens with lovers, when you feel them around you even when they are not actually there. How stupid I was. So, I was angry with Vineet, angrier than I have ever been with anybody, I think, and my blood boiled and boiled. I was also confused. I could not understand why he was doing all this. So I decided then and there, while sitting and eating lunch with Bobby, that I would meet Vineet as soon as I could and get some answers out of the man. But before I got up from the dining table, I looked at Bobby and, in a voice as cool and calm as Bobby's voice when he told me about meeting Vineet, I said, It is good that you met your Vineet Bhaiya, because he told me that from next week he is going to be out of station for some time.

⌒

I left the clinic one hour early yesterday and met Vineet at Barista in SDA. And what can I say? Vineet Sehgal lives in some other world. He does not think like normal people. Normal people who have affairs and who also have sense, and I think that means most people, normal people don't just leave everything, their husbands and children and homes, and run off with their lovers. But it seems that Vineet has no sense. I could not shout at him because there were so many people sitting around us, but when I asked him in the hardest but quietest way I could ask why he had been meeting Bobby without telling me, he just said, I am doing all this because I want to marry you.

Then he just kept begging me and begging me to marry him. He said that from his side everything is fine, it does not matter to him if I am a divorced woman, and that he has now also told his mother about me and she will also be fine. I almost laughed at this, and I wanted to tell him that he is the biggest fool in the world to think that his mother would treat a used woman with any type of respect, but I kept quiet. And then he told me that he knows me very well now, better than I know myself, he said, and he said that knowing the type of respectable woman that I am, I would never ever have started any relationship with another man if I was not already unhappy in my marriage, and that the only reason I have still not agreed to marry him is that I am scared about what will happen to Bobby, and now he, Vineet, wants to prove to me that he can look after Bobby.

I could not keep quiet any more. Look after Bobby? I said. You force my son to bunk school and then you say that you want to look after Bobby?

I did not force him to do anything, Vineet said. But even if I was a little stupid, even if I am not as mature as I am supposed to be, one thing I won't do is abandon him like his father did.

When he said this my head just burst. It seemed as if it had smashed into thousands of little, little pieces. I did not say anything for some time. It seemed as if I was trying to collect together all the broken pieces of my head. But after two or three minutes, I fixed my eyes on Vineet's eyes, and I said, Now, you listen to me very carefully, it is my turn to speak. And then very slowly and very calmly I said, In my family nobody abandons anybody. Bobby's father has not abandoned his son, he has not abandoned his wife, and he never ever will, and the opposite is also true. Bobby will not leave his father, and I will surely never ever leave my husband. Now, you better remember that.

Vineet's eyes roamed around the room but his mouth did not move.

And one last thing, I then said. You will swear on your mother that you will never ever meet my son again.

I have never sworn on my mother before, Vineet said, and I cannot swear on her now.

That is fine, I said, but remember that if you do ever dare to meet Bobby, then you will never see me again. And then I stood up and walked out of Barista.

⌐

When I had Skyped with my husband this morning he had said that there are two words that Arabs always use, inshallah, if God wills it, and khallas, finished. I can't say inshallah, because

God has not willed this relationship between Vineet and me, but I can say that it is khallas. Khallas, finished.

I am such a fool. I had always believed that Vineet was not interested in marriage at this stage in his life, but I had still made a promise to myself that if and when Vineet was ready to get married and his mother had found him a girl, then I would quietly walk away. I also believed that until that time for marriage came, Vineet and I could go on as it is. As long as Vineet behaved himself for the one month when my husband comes to Delhi each year, I thought that this relationship could last. And I also thought that if by chance Vineet was not interested in getting married at all, then this relationship could last for all the years that my husband is in Dubai, which would be at least another seven years if we want a good future for our son and ourselves.

But Vineet is interested in getting married, and even though he, and not his mother, has found the girl that he wants to marry and by chance that girl is me, even then I will not break my promise. Now I will walk away.

27

The straight road is not only the right road, but it is also actually the easier road to take. I know that in those five months with Vineet I would sometimes talk about how nice or calm or good I felt when I was with him, but the truth is that it was also difficult. People don't realise how difficult it is to have this type of relationship, which I will not call an affair because affairs mean sex, a lot of sex, and, actually, in all those five months Vineet and I had sex only three times and not one time more than that. But now that is all finished, the hiding, the lying, all those difficult times are all finished, khallas, and inshallah I will be on the straight road again.

Actually, maybe I am already on the straight road, because everything is already feeling better, less difficult, and nice things are starting to happen. The first and most important thing is that Bobby and I have made an agreement, a proper agreement that we talked about so seriously and carefully that I joked that we should get it attested at a notary public! Bobby has agreed to stop going to Ankit's father's restaurant, to study very hard and try to come in the first three ranks of his section as he always used to, and then to do an MBA. From my side, I have agreed to allow him to cook in the kitchen on all holidays, to also convince his grandmother to allow him to do that when she comes back, and to allow him to become a chef or whatever else he wants to become as long as he does his MBA first. Obviously I don't think that I actually have to worry about the last promise because after my Bobby has walked into a posh, fully air-conditioned office for his internship, Rosie told me that all MBA courses require students to do internships, would he then ever want to walk into a kitchen again? But yes, Bobby and I have made an agreement, and I think that we are both very happy about it.

Obviously Bobby wonders why Vineet has not called him up for so many days. Last evening Bobby told me that every time he has tried to call up Vineet, Vineet either does not pick up the phone or it is switched off. I said that Vineet is out of station, that he has gone off somewhere with Neha, and that maybe the network is poor in the place where he is, or the roaming charges are too high. I think that Bobby believes me because he has not talked about Vineet again.

Sometimes I think that Bobby is a lonely child. But that is the fate of an only child. Ask me. And that is why I am now trying to make Bobby become friendly with the girl with the green eyes at the bus stop. Actually, I don't have to make him become friendly with her. Every morning he picks up his dumbbells from next to the bed and does these funny exercises, and I know that it is just to impress her. I just have to help him. But we know her name now. It is Madhurima. I asked another mother at the bus stop.

A mother trying to help her son become friendly with a girl? I know that it sounds as if I have gone mad. But he is only fifteen years of age. What wrong can happen? I think that wrong things happen much more in the company of other boys. I cannot forget what happened the last two or three times that my son was with other boys. Either he came back home drunk or he came back home wanting to be a cook. And this Madhurima seems to be such a good, studious girl. It is obvious from the way her hair is tied neatly into a ponytail, from her bright white nicely pressed uniform, and from the way she stands quietly with her back straight and feet together, next to her father, waiting for her bus to come. And by looking at her father, it seems that she hails from a good family. Even at six thirty in the morning he is shaved and neatly dressed. And he drives a car. But obviously these things hardly matter. I am looking for a friend for my son, not a daughter-in-law.

So, as I said, nice things are happening, and on Monday another nice thing happened. I walked into Doctor Sahib's office between two of his appointments, I had decided that I should just walk straight in, and I greeted him and then I put down on his desk the shortlist of computer models that Vineet and Bobby and I had made, which I had obviously typed out neatly, and then and there Doctor Sahib asked me for a purchase order form, which I quickly brought, and then and there Doctor Sahib filled it out and signed it, and now, in ten days' time, there will be a new computer at the reception, which is only for me to use.

It is a little bit odd how these nice things have started to happen so suddenly. It seems as if these nice things had been standing quietly in line waiting for Vineet to go, waiting for Vineet to make some space for them, to make entry into my life again.

But the nicest thing of all is that my husband is coming back home in exactly one week's time. It is almost a little bit funny, but even though my husband is the one coming back home, I feel like I am also coming home. Have I gone mad?

But, yes, in one week's time, my husband will be here, and at exactly this time one week from now, my husband will be lying here next to me on this bed. On Sunday when we Skyped he looked better than he has ever, ever looked since he left me one year and nine months ago. He looked so happy and excited that even the computer monitor seemed to be brighter. I knew from his eyes and from the way he smiled that he had some plans for him and me that he could not tell me because Bobby was sitting just next to me. Still, he looked at me with that special look and he said, So, I hope the washing machine is working now. I looked back at him with the same look and said, Obviously it is.

I have already chosen the sari that I will wear to receive him at the airport. It is the orange and green Maheshwari that my mother-in-law bought for me last Diwali. I have only worn it one time, but I think that it suits me. I have also chosen a red collared t-shirt and navy-blue pants for Bobby. He will not wear a proper shirt, I know, and I don't want to get into any fights with him. But I have still not decided whether we should carry a garland for my husband or a bouquet of flowers. I don't want anything fancy, I don't want any drama at the airport. If it is a garland I was thinking of buying just a simple garland of marigolds. For the bouquet it would have to be roses, just one dozen roses, red or yellow, because in the summer months there is so little choice. I have also still not decided what I will say and do when I first see my husband. Should I just shake his hand? Or could I hug him? Maybe I could push Bobby in front of me and make him hug his father first, and then see if it is all right to do the same. And what should I say? You are looking very good, I could say. Or, How was the journey? One thing that I have done is to promise myself that I will not cry. No matter what happens, no matter how he looks or what he says, I will not allow myself to cry.

Maybe I could just greet him, then give him a very quick short hug, and then say, Fine, let's go, you must be very hungry.

28

I am wearing the orange and green sari that I had chosen for today, but I am not at the airport to receive my husband. I have kajal in my eyes and rouge on my cheeks and just a little bit of lipstick on my lips, but I am not at the airport. Only my son is. I am sitting in my flat. Dressed up like a bride I am sitting in the prayer room with a garland of marigolds on my lap and a dead man at my feet.

Six hours ago he was alive, this dead man. He was alive until the moment that I hit him on his head with my son's five-kilo dumbbell. Fifteen minutes before that he had entered into my house through the main door, without one knock, without one word. The main door was closed, but it was unlocked, because I always keep it unlocked in the afternoon so that my son can let himself in when he comes home from school. The man entered into my house quietly, and I don't know for how long he stood outside the kitchen watching me before he said, Renu, come with me now.

I jumped when I heard the voice. My heart jumped. I dropped the pot of rice that I was holding. What are you doing in my house? I said, trying not to shout.

He tried to come into the kitchen but I pushed him out into the hall. Get out of my house! I said. Now I was shouting. I did not care if the neighbours heard me.

I will only leave this house with you, he said.

My husband is coming back today, I said. Get out!

No! he said, also shouting now. You will come with me!

Then, for maybe eight or ten minutes, he shouted and he cried and he begged for me to leave my house and my husband and my life and go away with him. He would not stop. I tried everything to make him leave. I shouted loudly, I begged softly, I tried to explain everything to him, but the man refused to listen to me. He just kept shouting, crying, begging. Then suddenly he stopped. Suddenly, all the shouting and crying and begging stopped. Suddenly, for almost one full minute, I think, he was quiet, absolutely quiet. He sat down on the divan and looked down at his shoes.

I remained standing, leaning against the main door. The room was quiet. I could hear the tick-tick of the wall clock.

After a few seconds he stood up and looked around the room, then he looked at me and walked into my bedroom.

I tried to do some deep breathing. Please come out of that room, I said as calmly as I could say it. I was still standing against the main door. Please, I said again, very gently. Please come out, and let us sit down and talk to each other properly.

He did not say anything, but then suddenly I heard a sound, a sound like a thud, but not a very loud thud. Then I heard another soft thud, and then one more. When I reached the bedroom he looked up at me with the eyes of a madman.

You will never sleep on this bed again! he said, half-shouting, half-crying, hitting the bed with his fist, hitting the bed with his hand flat, thud, thud, thud, almost like my heart, actually, again and again with the strength of a madman. You will never ever sleep here again!

I tried to pull him away from the bed, but I just could not control him. This possessed madman just kept hitting the bed again and again while again and again he shouted, You will never ever sleep on this bed again!

Then suddenly he stopped and became quiet again. He bent down, and first I couldn't see what he was doing, but when he stood up, I saw that he had one of Bobby's five-kilo dumbbells in his hand. He turned his back to me and started looking around, and even though I could not see his face, I knew that he was looking for something to break. But these were our things, my family's things. I picked up the other dumbbell from the floor, and then, with all my strength, I hit him on the back of his head with it.

There and then he fell down. There and then he was dead.

❥

There were only around forty minutes left for Bobby to come back from school so I could not just sit there all day next to the body and cry. But it seemed as if I could not do anything else. It seemed as if my body could not move. Then I realised that until I calmed myself down there was nothing at all that I would be able to do. So I got up and went to the prayer room and closed my eyes and prayed, and then as my mind became calmer, my mind also became clearer, and then I understood what I had to do.

I went back to the bedroom. He still lay with his face down, the upper half of his body on the bed, his legs hanging off the bed, his feet on the floor. There was not much blood at all, just one small pool of blackish red at the back of his head and one thin stream of the same colour on the back of his shirt. That was all. I brought some water in a mug and cleaned the wound with my hanky. After that I covered it with gauze. I also tried to clean his shirt with a little bit of Surf. He did not look dead. He looked like a man who was either so tired or so drunk that he had fallen off to sleep while trying to get into bed.

After I cleaned him up nicely I had to pull him off the bed. He is not a very big man, not very heavy at all, but he was lying face down and I was scared that I would break his nose or his head if I just pulled him off the bed with his legs just like that. So I rolled him on to his back slowly and carefully, and then slowly and carefully I pulled him off the bed, inch by inch, with his legs. After that, after his whole body was on its back on the floor, I held on to his brown leather shoes and I pulled him into the prayer room. I have never carried a dead man but I always thought that the dead become heavy, become stone. But this was not very difficult, actually. Maybe because I make sure that the floor is always clean his body moved so smoothly, so easily across the floor as I pulled it. So I pulled him into the middle of the prayer room, under the fan, and straightened out his arms and legs. I tucked his shirt into his pants and smoothed his hair, and I switched on the fan. He was calm. Actually, I was also calm. Sitting next to him here in the prayer room I felt calm in the same way that I used to feel calm standing next to him on the Metro.

Then I remembered that I had to clean up everything before Bobby came back so I went back to the bedroom again. By God's grace there was not much cleaning up to do. There were some dents and scratches on the headboard and the right side of the bed, and some on the bedside table, but nothing else. I just had to straighten the bed sheet and pillows, and dust off the bedcover and spread it again neatly on the bed. After that I went to the kitchen to clean up the rice that had fallen on the floor.

It is an odd thing. I think that it did not take more than ten minutes for the house to look normal again. A man lost his life in this house, he got killed here, but just ten minutes after that this same house seemed normal again.

⌒

Before Bobby came back from school I had enough time to have a bath. But then I had to think, which was difficult, because I did not have to think like a mother or wife or daughter-in-law or receptionist, the people that I am. I had to think like a woman who has killed a man.

The first thing I thought was that Bobby should not know about this just now. He would know about it afterwards, but just now I should hide it from him. This, I knew, would be easy. He never goes into the prayer room, and if by chance he noticed the damage on the bed and bedside table, I would tell him that the pelmet came crashing down while I was cleaning the windows. Then I decided that I would send him alone to the airport to receive his father. I would tell him that I have had a very bad headache and that I would wait for them at home.

I don't know if I have thought correctly, I will only know that after some time, but killers probably never think correctly. But am I a killer if I never wanted to kill him?

⌐

I have sent Bobby off to the airport. I sent him off early. I told him to stop off at the flower seller in the market to buy a bouquet of roses for his father, yellow ones, one dozen of them, because I thought that I would keep the garland of marigolds that I had bought this morning to welcome my husband when he enters the flat. But the police will probably enter the flat before my husband will. So then maybe I will put the garland around the neck of the first policeman who enters the flat. Or maybe I will lay it over this dead body that lies here at my feet.

I will have to call up the police. There will be a smell soon. They will come, they will probably be here in forty-five minutes or one hour because the police are always late, and then they will be shocked. The police will be shocked to see such a respectable woman. They will look at each other, the three or four policemen who will come, and they will not know what to do with this woman who is so nicely dressed up in this pretty orange and green sari draped in the Gujarati style. What type of criminal is this? they will whisper to each other.

But am I actually a criminal? I did not want to kill him. I only wanted him to stop shouting and banging and breaking everything. My husband is coming back home. I only wanted this man to go away. Was that a crime?

His mother will think that it is a crime. Even if a tiger or cancer had killed her son, his mother would think that it is a crime.

But I will not lie to the police. I don't need to. They will understand. They will understand the reason why this respectable woman did what she had to do. They will investigate, and do blood tests and lie tests and what not. But it seems that they will have to arrest me first. That is the way it is, I think. I will be arrested before they do anything else. Maybe they will put handcuffs on me. And then after that they will investigate. And then they will understand.

My husband will also understand, I know. I am his wife. I can make him understand anything. Obviously he will first be angry. He will shout and he will cry and in the middle of all the drama my poor son will watch helplessly. But it will all be fine in the end, I know. Both these men know that I am a respectable woman.

But the mother won't understand.

⌒

I don't think that I am actually feeling too scared. The truth is that there is no reason to feel scared. And whatever it is, today is a special day, it is the day that my husband comes back to me after six hundred and nine days' time, and nobody, no dead body, no living body, is going to stop me, stop my family, from celebrating this grand day. I could not go to receive my husband at the airport, and I am sure that when he walks out of the airport building and sees his son standing there alone, his heart will break into a thousand little pieces, and maybe he is walking out just now, at exactly this moment, but even if I could not receive him at the airport, when he walks into his house today my husband will receive the grandest welcome from his wife. So the police will have to wait. If I call them just now, my husband and son are not going to get their dinner, and my husband has been waiting such a long time for this, and I don't like it when Bobby doesn't eat at the proper time. This man lying here will also have to wait because my husband and son will be here soon and they will be hungry, and even though the paneer and vegetables and dal are ready, and the dough is kneaded, I have to go into the kitchen now and make some more rice. This man will have to remain here lying quietly in the prayer room while we sit together, my husband and Bobby and I, after such a long time, and eat this delicious food that I have made.

What will my husband and son do when the police take me away? My husband doesn't know how to press his clothes properly. Who will cook? I know that Bobby can cook and I know how much he likes cooking, but he can only make all that fancy chef type of food. He can't make food for his family like a woman. And who will give Bobby his thyroid medicine?

Even my mother-in-law is not here, and anyway she is old. My husband will have to do everything then. He will not be able to go back to Dubai until I come back. He will not be able to go anywhere at all, actually. Rosie's husband will have to find him a new job. But that is after some time, after I come back. Just now my husband has to hold up the ceiling.

Acknowledgements

For her extraordinary constancy and unfailing support, I'd like to thank my agent, Bridget Wagner Matzie. For all the insight and energy they poured into this work, I want to thank Faiza S. Khan and all citizens of the Bloomsbury world. And finally, but foremostly, I'd like to thank Amitabha Bagchi: as ever, my wingman; as ever, near at hand.